Guarded Hearts

T. K. Conklin

Guarded Hearts

Butterfly Shadow Publishing
PO Box 182 Buffalo, Wyoming 82834

First Printing: February 2022

ISBN: 978-0-9986983-9-7
LCCN: 2022900808

Published in the United States of America

For Sally

Thank you for all the
encouragement and
shenanigans.

Chapter One

Rimrock, Wyoming Territory
Spring 1868

Mud squished beneath the hooves of the black horse as LaRisa rode toward the small town nestled in the valley at the base of the mountains. She gripped the reins tightly in her gloved hands and pulled in a deep breath to calm her nerves as her anxiety grew. Her emerald green eyes focused on the livery stable as she drew nearer. She didn't want to see the citizens' reaction when they saw her riding into town.

"We'll be fast, Saber," she told the big black-and-brown dog that trotted along slightly ahead of her horse.

LaRisa came to town every couple of months and had done so for over ten years, but the reaction from the citizens was still the same. Many feared her as a witch, and the stories had been exaggerated over the years. She brought herbs to the town doctor for him to use to help heal the good people who shunned her. Several of the townsfolk came to her cabin for certain herbs and even paid her extra to keep quiet about it.

She had lived alone since she was sixteen. She had no friends, had never been courted, and had accepted her life would always be this way. There were days when loneliness would set in, but she would visit her parents during those times. When she was in town delivering herbs to her uncle, she would see her aunt and cousins to help ease her loneliness. At twenty-seven and being feared by all, she knew the loneliness would forever be part of her life. No man wanted to court a witch.

"At least the other witches aren't afraid of me," she told her horse with little humor.

LaRisa's horse seemed to toss his head in agreement as he walked straight to the livery, knowing he would get fresh hay and time to rest before going home again. Saber sniffed at the corner of the building, then lifted a hind leg to urinate on the wood before heading for the open double doors.

Pulling her horse to a halt in front of the large, open livery door, LaRisa looked down the street. Many people stopped what they were doing to stare at her as others ducked into the nearest store to watch her through the window. Mothers turned their children from her view and hurried away. She could feel the hostile looks and almost hear the vile remarks. She hated coming to town.

"Afternoon, LaRisa," greeted a deep, friendly voice.

LaRisa looked to see a man with heavily muscled arms walking toward her from the blacksmith shop next to the livery. "Good afternoon, Roper."

"It's good to see you." He smiled a genuinely friendly smile at her. "You stayin' in town long?"

"You should know better than that," she told him as she dismounted. "I'll just be here long enough to see Sam." She moved to her saddlebags and removed a bundle wrapped in blue checked material.

"More herbs?" Roper asked.

She nodded. "I won't be long."

"I'm headed home for a bite to eat. Stop by before you leave. I'm sure that Marie would be happy to see you."

LaRisa nodded, though she knew she wouldn't be stopping by her cousin's house today.

Roper bid her a good day and headed down the street. She sighed. Roper was such a nice man, and Marie had done right by marrying him. LaRisa was glad the women in her family had found kind and understanding men that loved them for who they were and accepted what they could do.

Her eyes moved to the blacksmith shop, and she bit her bottom lip. She cast a quick glance at her horse's hooves. He didn't really need new shoes, but…she summoned her courage and led him to the shop. Saber darted from the livery to follow her, panting happily.

She stopped and scanned the area. The bellows were quiet, and there was no hammering or swearing. She felt a surge of disappointment and figured he was off to lunch as well. If she was brave, she would check back later. New shoes for her horse were a logical reason to see a blacksmith. Even if he didn't really need them. She turned and led her horse into the livery.

"Quinn? Jonny?" she called when she entered, but there was no answer. "Everyone must be out for lunch," she told her horse.

LaRisa walked down the row of stalls until she found an empty one. Saber ran through the livery, sniffing and inspecting every nook and cranny for mice or a cat to chase.

Setting her bundle down on a hay bale, she turned to the task of unsaddling her horse. Though she intended to leave town as quickly as possible, she did need a few things and would be in town a couple of hours. So when she felt brave enough, she would head to the general store and place an order for supplies.

Brave. Why did she have to work up courage to do anything? Because everyone in town was afraid of her, and she didn't enjoy being around people. Sometimes she feared they would pack her off to the nearest wood pile and set her on fire.

"Sometimes I wonder if it would be easier to just let them send me off in a puff of smoke," she told Blackie as she loosened the cinch. He only tossed his head and blew through his nose. "Some help you are."

"Miss Reeves?"

LaRisa yelped and whirled to face the man standing behind her. She placed a gloved hand over her racing heart in an attempt to calm it. She couldn't find her voice as she stared at the man towering over her. Though she had been around him a handful of times, it still took her a moment to get used to his hulking presence. She had always thought herself tall for a woman, but his broad and very solid frame made her feel small and more fragile than she liked. Or maybe she *did* like it. Her eyes flicked to the well-worn gun on his hip. *That* she did not like.

"Hello, Mr. Strykes," she managed to say, though her voice shook. Even though she had been looking for him only a moment ago, she wasn't prepared to see him now.

"I didn't mean to startle you." His voice was deep and had a drawl to it. She found it oddly soothing.

She huffed out a breath of irritation. "Well, you did," she informed him, absently pulling at the gloves she wore.

"Want me to take care of your horse?" He nodded toward the animal.

"You?"

He nodded. "Quinn and Jonny are helping the marshal with a prisoner transfer. I'm looking after things."

"Oh," she said quietly. Saber appeared at her side, and she reached down to stroke his head.

That explained why Strykes wasn't at the blacksmith's shop. Jonny and Quinn often helped the marshal, so it shouldn't have been a surprise to see Strykes in the livery.

"Want me to take care of your horse?" he asked again in that low drawl of his.

She looked at her horse as if she had forgotten the animal was even there. "Uh, yes." She faced him again. "Yes, that would be fine. I only plan on being in town an hour or so."

He nodded. "Just give a holler when you're ready to leave, and I'll saddle him up for you."

"Thank you," she said hastily and brushed past him, Saber padding after her.

She was halfway through the livery when she remembered the herbs for Doc Sam. She turned on her heel to head back and ran into something solid. She stumbled backward, and a powerful arm went around her to hold her steady. She blinked up into the clear, almost colorless blue eyes of Strykes. The eyes looked so pale next to his tan skin and black hair and mustache.

Saber's low, protective growl pulled her from her staring. "Sorry."

"You all right?" he asked, his deep voice holding a hint of humor.

She nodded and busied herself with smoothing down the front of her dress. "Fine."

"You forgot this." He held out the cloth-covered bundle to her.

"I know," she said quickly and took it from him. "Thank you."

Unsure of what else to say, LaRisa turned on her heel and walked briskly away, her dog following. The feel of his arms around her lingered. She had never been in a man's arms before. Well, except her father when she was a child, but that didn't count. And though Strykes hadn't touched her skin, she seemed to tingle where his arms had been. So many unfamiliar feelings went through her.

LaRisa decided that the best thing to do was take care of her business in town and get home as fast as she could. She would give Sam the herbs. Then go to the general store and leave her list with Toby. The aging man would drop her things off later in the day, and she could get back to her normal life.

She scoffed, knowing her life was far from normal and that Strykes would plague her mind for the rest of the day. More so than he already did.

***

Strykes let the chuckle he had been holding back rumble in his chest when LaRisa had left. He pulled out his makings and rolled himself a smoke as he watched her walk down the street. Her auburn hair was in a thick braid down her back, the sun dancing off the many shades of red, and the simple green calico dress swayed as she walked. She moved gracefully, she practically glided, and he liked to watch her. Her emerald eyes fascinated him. They were beautiful but haunted, and he often wondered about that.

He lit his cigarette and took a long drag as he shook out the match and flicked it into the dirt. LaRisa never came to town often, but when she did, it was always a treat to his eyes. During the winter, he had seen little of her, but now it was spring and she was making more trips to town. Bringing a small amount of pleasure to his dreary life. He had been fascinated by her the very first time he had seen her. A small smile tugged his mouth at the memory of their first meeting last year.

He frowned as he watched the townspeople avoid walking too close to her. Some stared, others whispered to one another, some crossed the street to avoid her altogether.

LaRisa walked briskly, careful not to look at anyone as she passed. That happened every time she came to town, and he imagined it had to do with the rumor that she was a witch. Just because she kept to herself and grew healing herbs didn't make her a witch.

Only when she disappeared into Doc Sam's clinic did Strykes turn and head back for her horse. The black horse had found his way to a pile of hay and was eating happily. Strykes took the reins and led him to the empty stall. He removed the saddle and bridle from the animal before tossing in hay and closing the stall gate.

Strykes picked up the saddle and bridle to carry them to the tack room for the time being. When LaRisa's gear was put away, Strykes headed back to the blacksmith's shop. He had a wagon wheel to fix.

Chapter Two

Though his mind was filled with LaRisa, Strykes somehow managed to get the wagon wheel repaired. Now he stood in his small room in the back of the blacksmith shop, washing up. He didn't want her seeing him filthy. He wasn't sure why it mattered; she had been to the shop many times and had seen him covered in dirt, soot, and grease.

Strykes stared at his reflection in the mirror. His nearly colorless blue eyes looked back at him with no expression. His father's eyes. Oh, how he would love to pluck them from his face. Taking a deep breath, he closed his eyes and shook his head. He might hate his eyes, but he needed them. He might hate the fact that he looked like the man who had raised him, but there was nothing he could do about that. The key was not to become his father.

He opened his eyes again to study his reflection in the mirror and thought back over his life, once again thankful that he had been given a second chance instead of getting hung or rotting in prison. It was amazing how his life had turned completely around. Yet underneath the black-smudged, dirty, sweat-streaked face, he was still the same man.

Every day, the need to drift across the country was strong, but he always pushed it down. The need to go home was stronger, but he no longer had a home. The war had taken that from him and his family. He had sent his sisters to New Orleans to live with an aunt, and the war had swallowed him up. Strykes longed to see them, but he didn't want them to know the kind of man he had become. He had considered letting them think he had been killed in the war, but not wanting them to feel that hurt, he sent them a letter when he had settled in Rimrock. Instead, he would let them think he was a decent man living a normal life.

This simple life he was living in the present couldn't erase what he had done in the past. He couldn't forget all that had happened to him, and at the same time, he didn't want to forget. He had learned so much in those many years. Years of blood, pain, and death. Too much blood, pain, and death. The killing should have stopped after the war, but it hadn't. Hell, the killing had started long before the war.

He took another deep breath and let it out slowly. He filled his hands with water and splashed it over his face, enjoying the feel of the cool water on his skin. Strykes felt the all-too-familiar feeling of being watched. He splashed water over his face again and tried to shake off the feeling. He was too edgy. There was no reason to feel that way here. His past was just that—the past. Why couldn't he remember that? He picked up the soap and washed his face and arms.

When the water was good and dirty, Strykes straightened and reached for the towel. A movement reflected in the mirror, and his hand flashed for the gun at his hip in an easy, practiced move. There was a gasp as he whirled and aimed the gun at the figure in the doorway. He stared into a pair of wide, frightened emerald eyes.

"Mr. Strykes," LaRisa stammered. "I just came for my horse."

Strykes let out his breath and lowered the pistol. "Jesus, LaRisa. I'm sorry. I didn't know it was you."

"Thank you for not shooting me," she said in a shaky breath.

"Sorry," he told her again as he ran a wet hand through his hair. "Old habits die hard." He dropped the pistol back into his holster and finished drying his face.

"Yes, well, it's been a while since you've had to shoot anyone. I sure don't want it to be me," she pointed out as she tugged her gloves tightly to her fingers. "And if you do get in a gunfight, I really don't want to have to patch you up again."

"As I recall, it was a rather pleasant experience," Strykes told her evenly as he dried his hands. "Aside from the bullet holes in me."

LaRisa's face heated as she fidgeted with her gloves, and he knew she was remembering back when he had shown up at her cabin with her cousin Leslie. He had been shot helping Leslie escape from a gang of outlaws. Leslie had brought him to LaRisa seeking help, and he knew he would never forget the first time he had seen LaRisa. She had answered the door in her nightdress, and her hair was loose, falling around her shoulders and down her back in beautiful auburn waves.

"I'll get your horse," he said as he tossed the towel down and walked past her, a bit closer than necessary to brush against her, and headed toward the stables.

LaRisa had done an amazing job of getting him patched up and on his way again. He had touched her hair as she tended his wounds, and it had felt like silk as he ran it through his fingers. When she hadn't protested, he had let his fingers trail over her cheek, and her skin had been so soft.

She had fascinated him from the first moment he laid eyes on her, and he still looked at her as often as he could. Just the sight of her made his heart pound in his chest, and unfamiliar feelings washed over him. He had never felt the need to be close to anyone before, yet he had the feeling he could never be close enough to her. That feeling alone was reason enough to keep his distance from her.

LaRisa had composed herself by the time Strykes returned with her horse. Her dog sat at her side, his dark eyes watching Strykes warily. He shot the dog a scowl, and the animal's lips curled slightly in a silent snarl.

"Thank you, Mr. Strykes," she said simply as she took the reins from him.

"You're welcome, Miss Reeves," Strykes drawled, and she stood there staring at him for a long moment. "Yes?"

It startled her from her staring, and her cheeks heated again. "Shoes," she blurted.

"Shoes?"

"D-does he need new shoes?" she asked, though she sounded breathless.

Strykes fought a grin and took his time checking her horse's shoes. "They look fine," he said when he finished. "Bring him back in a couple weeks." He knew the horse could go longer than a couple of weeks, but he wanted to see her again.

"Thank you," she said with a nod and prepared to mount.

"You're welcome." He put his hands on her waist to help her into the saddle. She didn't need the help, but he wanted to touch her.

When she was seated, she smoothed her trembling hands over her dress. "Thank you again." She glanced at him and met his eyes for a moment before she kicked her horse and rode out.

Strykes walked to the livery doors and watched her ride down the street, the dog trotting beside the horse. She sat her horse confidently but was careful not to look at any of the townspeople. He hoped she would come to town again soon. He should have lied to her and said a few days instead of a few weeks.

"You gonna stand there all day?" Roper asked from behind him.

Strykes turned and glared at his friend. "You just don't worry about what I'm doing."

Roper laughed as they walked to the blacksmith's shop. "Don't let her pa catch you looking at her like that."

Strykes didn't want to think of what Matthew Reeves might do to him if the man knew he was lusting after his daughter. "Don't worry; he never will."

Disappointment and frustration washed over him. No matter how much he wanted to court LaRisa, he knew it was something that he couldn't let happen. But he had a feeling it was going to be harder than hell to keep his distance. Maybe for her safety, he should drift on to a different town.

"I'm going to go out back and work on Doc's buggy," Roper told him.

Strykes only grunted as he went to the bellows and pumped them, staring at the coals as they glowed red. Using pincers, he placed a length of iron into the coals. He watched as it heated and did his best not to think of LaRisa. It was impossible.

His mind was plagued with thoughts of her as he stood at the anvil with hammer in hand. Each time he brought it down on the iron, sparks flew as the piece flattened. He enjoyed the labor and got satisfaction in creating things with his hands.

"Hello," a man called.

Strykes looked up from shaping shoes to see Logan McCord ride up on his black appaloosa. The animal's rump was blanketed white with black spots. Logan was leading a tired-looking sorrel horse behind him. Knowing Logan took good care of his horses, Strykes felt curiosity fill him. How had he acquired such a worn-out animal? He placed the hammer and piece of iron down to approach the young man.

"Buy a new horse?" Strykes inquired as Logan dismounted.

"Nope. Found him wandering around my place," he said simply. "Brought him in to see if anyone in town has been asking after him. Boone told me to bring him over here to keep for a while."

Strykes nodded. "I'll take care of him. Looks like he could use a few days of rest and grain."

Logan's gray eyes moved over the sorrel. "Someone used him hard. I don't recognize the brand, but Boone was going to check into it and see if he can come up with where he might have come from."

Strykes took the lead of the sorrel from Logan. "I'll let him know if anyone comes looking for the horse."

"Thanks, Strykes." Logan mounted his horse again. "Have a good day."

Strykes led the horse into the livery and to an empty stall. The tired animal put up no objection. Strykes tossed him hay and brushed him down. The sorrel was a good-looking horse, and once he was rested and well, he would be quite a prize.

Running the brush over the brand on the horse's hip, Strykes paused and looked at it for a long time. The brand was familiar to him, but he couldn't place it.

A memory nudged at his mind, but he couldn't grasp it. Whatever it was, Strykes knew it wasn't a good memory.

Chapter Three

LaRisa took a deep breath as she dismounted in front of the blacksmith's shop. New shoes for her horse were still a good reason to see him. Besides, he had told her to bring her horse back in a couple of weeks. She was a week early, but maybe he wouldn't notice.

The sound of a hammer hitting metal echoed in the air. She stepped closer to the building and peeked around the corner. She saw Strykes standing at the bellows, shaping shoes. His big hand held the hammer easily, and the muscles in his arms and chest bulged against his shirt. She bit her lip and watched him for a long moment.

She probably would have stood there all day watching him if her horse hadn't given a loud snort and shoved at her with his nose. She stumbled slightly and glared at him. The hammering stopped, and she turned to see Strykes looking right at her.

"Miss Reeves," he greeted as he placed the hammer and shoe down. "Can I help you?" he asked as he walked toward her.

LaRisa felt her face heat, and she did her best to compose herself. "Yes," she said, hoping she sounded professional. "I brought my horse in for new shoes," she told Strykes, as she led the black horse from behind the building. She saw his mouth twitch as if he might smile, but none came.

"Good timing. I was just getting his shoes ready."

She blinked at him. "You were?"

He gave her a half smile. "I had a feeling you'd be early."

She felt her face flush, and she handed him the reins of her horse as she averted her eyes. "I had to come to town today anyway," she lied.

His eyes glanced around quickly before he looked at her again. "No dog?"

She shook her head. "No, I left him behind to guard the garden. Rabbits have been trying to eat everything."

"I bet he wasn't happy."

"No, he wasn't," she told him and couldn't help the small smile as she thought of her dog sitting on the porch, pouting as she rode away.

Strykes studied her for a moment before he spoke. "Would you like to have lunch with me today?"

Her eyes widened, and her mouth fell open and she stared at him as if he had lost his mind.

"It's just lunch at Milly's," he told her, and she just stared at him. "You don't have to look so horrified. I do have manners," he assured her.

LaRisa blinked at him and did her best to compose herself. "I'm sure you do."

He wanted to take her to lunch, and she had no idea how to answer him. Nobody had ever asked her to go to lunch before. Nobody had ever asked her to do anything. Everyone was afraid of her and never wanted to be seen with her in public.

The thought of having lunch with him terrified her. Not just the fact of being with him, but she would be in the café with many other people, and she didn't know if she could tolerate the looks they would give her. She would be uncomfortable, and he would be lucky if anyone spoke to him again for having lunch with a witch.

He looked at her expectantly. "LaRisa?"

She swallowed hard. "I-I can't," she managed to say and felt her spirits sink. She had been looking forward to seeing him, and now that she was here, she wanted to run away. She couldn't read his expression, but his eyes had gone cold. "Th-the shoes can wait," she told him as she reached for her reins.

Strykes saw the fear in her eyes as she tried to take the reins from him, but he held them tight. He almost swore out loud. He knew his size was intimidating, and he wasn't a friendly person, but he didn't want her to be afraid of him.

Though he knew being afraid of him was probably the only thing that would keep her safe *from* him. Yet it wasn't as if they would be alone, and she didn't have to fear for her virtue. They would be in the café, for Christ's sake. She tugged at the reins, but he didn't let go.

"I have to go," she told him and heard the tremble in her voice.

He let out a long breath. "Forget about lunch then," he told her. "I'll just shoe your horse, and you can go on about your business."

The harsh tone of his voice made her look at him, and she blurted, "I can't go to the café."

He studied her for a moment. "Why?"

"I-I just can't," she said and released the reins. "I'm sorry." She wasn't sure why she apologized to him for it. "I'll be back," she told him and turned away before he could ask her any questions.

Strykes moved to the side of her horse and leaned an arm on the saddle as he watched her hurry away. Why couldn't she go to the café? He thought about that for a moment and could come up with no logical explanation why she couldn't. Everyone went to Milly's to eat now and again; in fact, he ate most of his meals there. Usually he was alone, and the idea of her joining him had been very appealing.

A smile tugged at his mouth. She might not want to have lunch at Milly's, but she didn't say she didn't want to have lunch with *him*.

He watched her dash to the doctor's house as he made a plan. She didn't want to go to Milly's. Then he would just have to bring the café to her.

***

LaRisa flung open the door to the clinic and shut it quickly behind her. She leaned her back against the door and tried to catch her breath. Strykes had asked her to lunch. That still shocked the hell out of her. After all, she did like him and should have been flattered instead of terrified.

Sam came from his office. "LaRisa, are you all right?"

She let out a long breath. "I don't know."

He gave her a look of concern and stepped forward. "Are you feeling ill?"

"No," she blurted. "I just had a shock." She took a deep breath and stood up straight. "I'm fine."

He gave her a skeptical look but didn't ask any more questions. "I wasn't expecting you today."

"I didn't plan on stopping in today, but I guess I changed my mind," she said in way of explanation.

He eyed her suspiciously. "Are you sure you're fine?"

"Yes. Since I'm here," she said, trying to regain her composure, "are there any herbs you're running low on?"

Sam went along with her change of subject, and she was grateful. She followed him into the examination room and waited patiently as he looked over the jars of herbs on the shelf. He gave her a list of the herbs he needed, and she promised to deliver them in a few weeks.

Not wanting to leave yet, she inquired about her aunt. Sam informed her that True was home and to go visit. She didn't hesitate as she moved to the door that separated Sam's house from the clinic.

"Aunt True?" LaRisa called as she entered the house.

"In here," her voice came from the kitchen.

LaRisa entered the room to find her aunt elbow deep in bread dough. "Looks like you're having fun."

True smiled at her, her dark eyes sparkling. "Are you staying for lunch?"

Another invitation to lunch. "No," she said with a shake of her head. "I just came to visit you."

True blinked at her, surprise clear on her face. "You did?"

LaRisa let out a long breath and sank down into a kitchen chair. "Truth is, I brought my horse in for shoes, and I don't want to be in town. I'm hiding."

True laughed as she kneaded the dough. "Feel free to hide here anytime you want."

LaRisa smiled at her aunt. She should visit more often, but she never felt comfortable around people. She loved her family dearly, and they all treated her as if she were normal.

Of course, none of the women in her family were truly normal. They all had things they hid from the rest of the town. She felt a wave of sadness wash over her; she had more to hide than most.

Brushing off her self-pity, she listened to her aunt fill her in on the happenings of her family. Her daughter was about to have a baby, and she was overly excited.

LaRisa liked her cousin Leslie. The two had been inseparable while they were growing up, but that was before LaRisa's life had changed and she had chosen to isolate herself from the rest of the world. It seemed like so very long ago, yet she remembered it all like it was yesterday.

LaRisa spent a couple of hours with her aunt. True did most of the talking, and Sam soon joined them. They talked and reminisced about the family. She noted they were careful to leave certain people and events out. She knew it was to put her at ease, yet all knew the memories were in all of their minds. The death of Sam's father would forever haunt LaRisa.

When she thought a safe amount of time had passed, she bid them good afternoon and made her way back to the blacksmith's shop. She took a deep, calming breath as she headed toward the building. All she had to do was pay Strykes and get her horse. Nothing hard about that. Only when she got to the shop, she didn't see Strykes or her horse anywhere. The bellows were quiet, and she made her way through the building.

"Mr. Strykes," she called. "I came for my horse."

"Back here," he answered.

She followed the sound of his voice and found him behind the building. She stared in disbelief at the red-checked tablecloth draped over a couple of boards lying on two sawhorses. A basket sat in the middle of the makeshift table, and there were two places set. Two stumps served as chairs, and she could only stare. Her eyes moved to him, and the corner of his mouth moved in a slight smile. He had washed up and had clean clothes on.

"You said you didn't want to go to the café," he told her as he stepped up to her. "So I brought the café to you."

LaRisa couldn't speak, and she could hardly breathe as she took it all in. Nobody had ever done anything like this before. She wanted to run away, but she didn't see her horse anywhere; she guessed Strykes had planned it that way. With no other choice, she went with him as he gestured her to a stump, and she sat down.

"I went to the café and had Kelly make us something," he told her as he unloaded the basket.

LaRisa watched as he set out the food before he sat on his own stump across from her. She felt her eyes burn and had to blink the threat of tears away. Why would he do this for her? He barely knew her, yet he had been the only person outside her family to treat her like a human being. She just figured it was because he hadn't been in town long and didn't know any better.

"Are you all right?"

She swallowed hard. "I think so."

"I wasn't sure what you liked, so I had Kelly surprise us," he told her as he filled his plate.

LaRisa tried to keep her hands from shaking as she dished out her own food. Kelly was an excellent cook, and everything tasted wonderful. She could feel his clear blue eyes on her, and she tried not to look at him. They ate in mostly silence. She hardly knew him, and he appeared content just to have her company.

"That was good," he said when he had finished.

She nodded. "It was." She stood and gathered up the dirty dishes. "I should be heading home." She carefully placed everything back into the basket.

Strykes said nothing as he got to his feet and walked into the livery to get her horse. He saddled the animal, unsure how to feel about his lunch with LaRisa. She hadn't said over two words, and all he could do was stare at her. She had eaten quickly and was now eager to be gone from him. At least she had stayed and eaten with him. That was something. He led her horse through the livery and back outside to where she waited.

"Here you go," he told her, and she wasted no time taking the reins from him.

LaRisa put a foot in the stirrup and paused. "Mr. Strykes." She turned her head and finally looked at him. "Thank you for lunch."

He gave her a slight smile and felt an unexpected feeling wash over him. A feeling he couldn't quite place. "It was my pleasure, Miss Reeves."

She turned her attention back to mounting, and he placed his hands on her waist to help her into the saddle. She cast him one last look before she rode around the building and disappeared. Strykes smiled and leaned back against the makeshift table. It wobbled, and he straightened. He had seen the smile playing on LaRisa's lips before she had ridden out. Even if it didn't appear so, she had enjoyed herself, and he was sure going to do this again with her.

His smile faded as he thought of their lunch together. What the hell had he been thinking? He liked her and wanted to spend time with her. That alone could be a big problem. He had no business liking a woman, especially one as perfect as LaRisa. The next step would be obsession, and he couldn't let that happen.

Chapter Four

LaRisa watched as Mr. Clark and his son, Lloyd, placed the roll of wire and a dozen fence posts into her wagon. She knew fencing her garden was something she should have done years ago, but she had lacked the ambition to do it. As well as lacking supplies.

"This will work wonderfully," she told the older man. "Thank you."

Mr. Clark wasn't a rich man but needed her herbs to help with his wife's headaches, as well as his own pain when the weather changed. In exchange for the herbs, he had given her the fencing supplies.

The Clarks were one of many families that sought her out for her healing herbs. Though in public they didn't acknowledge her, they were pleasant enough in private. Lloyd, however, was still leery of her and stared at her constantly. She supposed the teenager had heard many elaborate stories about the witch.

"We appreciate your medicine," Mr. Clark told her as he closed the tailgate of the wagon. "Bessie wouldn't be able to do much without it. Her spells are coming more frequently."

LaRisa nodded in understanding. "Just send Lloyd for more when she needs it."

LaRisa gathered her dress and climbed up into the seat of the wagon. She picked up the reins and nodded to the two men before urging her horse toward the road.

She gave a heaving sigh. She wasn't looking forward to the labor involved with building the fence around her garden. Maybe she would get her brother to help her. She smiled as she thought of the groan of protest Tim would give her before he agreed to help.

The wheel dropped in a rut, and the wagon lurched and bounced. Something under the wagon snapped. She looked back to see the wagon bed tilting to the left.

"Great," she grumbled as she faced forward again. "A broken spring."

It was going to be a rougher ride than normal going home. One more thing to fix. A smile curved her mouth.

"Looks like we need to go to town tomorrow, Blackie." Her smile widened. "A broken spring is a good reason to pay the blacksmith a visit."

***

Strykes heard a wagon rattle up to the blacksmith's shop. He paused in making nails to look up. His heart picked up a notch when he saw LaRisa pull the wagon to a stop.

As always, she was beautiful. Her hair was in a long braid, and today she wore a wide-brimmed straw hat to protect her flawless skin from the sun. Her blue dress hugged her figure in a way that made his hands ache with the need to touch her.

Strykes put the hammer aside and walked to LaRisa's wagon. "Good afternoon, Miss Reeves."

Much to his pleasant surprise, she favored him with a bright smile. He was even more surprised when he smiled back at her. He wasn't sure how long they stood there staring at each other, but her horse snorted and tossed his head.

Strykes swore as he wiped horse snot from his cheek, and LaRisa laughed. It was a beautiful sound, and Strykes wished he could hear it every day.

"Sorry," LaRisa said, and did her best to stifle her giggles. "I shouldn't laugh."

"Yes, you should. I like it," he told her before he could stop himself.

She blushed and focused on securing the reins around the brake lever. "I need you to take a look at my wagon. I think one of the springs is broken in the back."

"I'll see what I can do," he told her as he reached up to help her from the wagon seat.

"Thank you," she said as he set her on her feet. She stepped back and absently smoothed at her dress with her gloved hands.

LaRisa reached into the floor of the wagon and pulled out a basket covered with a green cloth. Strykes imagined it was herbs for Doc Sam. She had been making more trips to town than normal to provide the doctor with healing herbs.

"Saber guarding the garden again?" he asked, noticing the absence of the big dog.

She nodded. "Yes, and he's not happy about it."

Strykes chuckled softly. "I don't imagine he is."

She gave him another smile, and a long silence stretched between them. Her slender fingers nervously fidgeted with the handle of the basket she carried.

He cleared his throat. "I better see to your horse and wagon."

"Yes," she said quickly and a bit loudly.

LaRisa's cheeks heated, and she abruptly turned and hurried away. Strykes couldn't help but smile. He had never seen her behave this way before. It was cute.

His smile faded. She had changed toward him since their picnic out behind the livery. Was she developing feelings for him? His smile brightened as he led the horse behind the blacksmith shop and unhitched him.

After turning the black horse out into the corral, he inspected her wagon. As LaRisa suspected, one of the wagon springs was broken. It would probably only take him a couple of hours to fix.

First, he had horses to feed. Walking into the livery, Strykes picked up the pitchfork and went to the pile of fresh hay. The horses nickered at him, eager for their meal.

"Afternoon."

Strykes looked up to see Boone Cain coming toward him. The sun glinted off the badge on his chest. Never in a million years would Strykes have thought the man would put on a badge, even if it was only until the marshal returned.

Boone's past was just as questionable as his own, and they both had done their fair share of illegal things. The only thing that kept them from hanging was there was no proof.

Strykes smirked at him. "Come to arrest me, Cain?"

Boone laughed and shook his head. "Unfortunately, no. But I'm looking forward to the day I get to."

"You'll be waiting a long time. I put that life behind me. Just like you did."

Boone's face grew serious. "Yeah, we left it behind, but I'm afraid, it caught up to us."

Strykes set aside the pitchfork and gave Boone his full attention. "What are you talking about?"

"That horse." He gestured to the sorrel two stalls down. "The brand is from a ranch in Missouri."

Something in Strykes's stomach tightened. "Missouri?"

"Yeah, he was stolen a few months ago, along with a gray and a buckskin. The man that took them was an average-height blond man in his late twenties." Boone's blue eyes held a knowing that Strykes didn't like. "His left hand was missing two fingers—pinky and ring finger—and he had a limp."

"Left leg?" Strykes asked, though he knew the answer.

Boone nodded sagely. "From when you shot him. And if a horse he stole has been found around Rimrock, I'd say Lucas is back for you."

He met Boone's eyes evenly. "And you."

"Yeah."

"How many men do you think he'll have with him?"

Boone thought for a moment. "At least a dozen. He's too chickenshit to do anything on his own. Probably a few of Fisher's gang that we didn't kill or catch last year."

"And they'll want revenge too," Strykes muttered as his mind worked. "I knew we should have gone after them."

"*We* weren't in any condition to be going anywhere," Boone told him flatly. "I'd been shot, died, and came back to life. You were shot full of holes."

"Just two," he muttered.

The wounds had kept him from going after Lucas that day Boone had nearly died. *Had* died, according to Boone and Leslie.

"We'll keep our eyes open for them," Boone said. "Travis, Quinn, and Jonny will be back soon, and I'll feel a lot better about this then."

"Me too," he admitted, even though he didn't want to. "You better stay close to Leslie. It's because of her, most of Fisher's gang was killed and she ruined their plans. Lucas won't forget that."

"I'll keep her safe." Worry for his wife was clear.

"Did you tell Heck about this?" Strykes wasn't sure how the deputy marshal would feel about trouble coming to town again.

Boone nodded. "I did, and he wasn't too thrilled about it."

"Suppose he'll run us out of town before there's any trouble?"

"I'm not going anywhere," Boone said flatly. "Leslie's about to have a baby, and I won't leave her. This is our home, and I'll be damned if I let someone like Lucas run me out. And you sure as hell aren't going anywhere. I need you here to watch my back."

A small smile tugged Strykes's mouth. "I guess someone has to. You can't seem to take care of yourself."

Boone grinned at him. "You've helped me out of a few scrapes, and I'd hate to have that change now."

Strykes nodded. "So I'll watch your back and you'll watch mine."

"That's right. I got too much to live for to die now."

Strykes wished he could say the same, but he had no desire to get killed either. Boone had a wife and a baby on the way. He had put his old ways behind him and settled into the family life easily. Strykes had a respectable job, and that was about all he had going for him. His mind drifted to LaRisa and wished he could have a life with her. The thought both pleased him and scared the hell out of him.

"Strykes, you all right?" Boone asked, his expression one of concern.

Shaking off his thoughts, he nodded. "Yeah, fine."

Boone clearly didn't believe him but didn't press further. "I'll keep you informed if I learn anything about where Lucas might be."

"I'll do the same," Strykes said absently.

They bid each other good day, and Boone left Strykes to his thoughts. Strykes turned to look at the sorrel horse in the stall for a moment. Walking to the stall, he studied the animal as he ate his hay. The horse with the 3 broken bar 7 branded on his hip had been stolen by Lucas and left here for Strykes and Boone as a warning.

If Lucas was in the area, it would be only a matter of days before he struck. He would give Boone and Strykes enough time to find out where the horse came from, let them worry, and set them on edge. Lucas would wait until he felt both men were worked up and impatient for the coming fight and move in, hoping that Boone and Strykes would make a bad choice from impatience, and then he would kill them.

A small smile tugged his mouth. Lucas was in for a long wait. Both Strykes and Boone knew how the man thought, and with no reaction from them, Lucas would become the impatient one.

This time, Strykes intended to put a bullet in his heart. He had made the mistake of only wounding Lucas last time; he wouldn't make the same mistake twice.

***

LaRisa opened the door to the boardinghouse and stepped in. "Hello?" she called as she closed the door softly behind her.

"LaRisa?"

Footsteps sounded from the kitchen, and Leslie appeared in the doorway. A wide smile formed on Leslie's mouth as her face brightened with happiness. Her dark eyes sparkled as she approached her cousin.

LaRisa returned her smile. "I hope you don't mind me dropping in."

"Oh, heavens, no." Leslie reached out and hugged LaRisa, her pregnant belly hindering the act slightly. "Come in, I made tea."

LaRisa followed her cousin into the kitchen and dining area to sit at the table. Leslie poured them each a cup of tea before joining LaRisa.

"What brings you by today?" Leslie asked as she sipped her tea.

LaRisa fidgeted with her cup. "Strykes is fixing my wagon, and I thought I'd visit until he was finished."

A small knowing smile tugged Leslie's mouth. "Is your horse getting new shoes as well?"

"No." She felt the blush wash over her cheeks.

"You like Strykes, don't you?"

She nodded. "He asked me to have lunch at Milly's with him last time I was in town."

"He did! Did you go?"

She shook her head. "I couldn't. People will treat him different if they see him with me."

Leslie sighed and reached out to touch LaRisa's gloved hand. "No, they won't. You have to stop thinking everyone is afraid of you."

She felt the tears burn her eyes as she looked at Leslie. "But they *are* afraid of me."

"Strykes isn't."

"That's because he hasn't been in town long."

Leslie scoffed as she sat back. "Nonsense. It's because he likes you. A lot."

A humorless laugh left LaRisa. "He does not." She hesitated a moment. "Do you really think so?"

Leslie smiled. "Yes. He asked you to lunch, didn't he?"

"But I told him I couldn't. When I went back to get my horse, Strykes had gone to the café and gotten a basket of lunch for us. We ate together at the livery."

Leslie smiled brightly. "See? He does like you. I think he liked you the moment he met you."

LaRisa said nothing as she took a drink of tea. She had to admit, she hadn't liked Strykes all that much when they had first met. He had been part of the outlaw gang that had kidnapped Leslie a year ago. Strykes had a change of heart and helped Leslie escape. Getting shot in the process.

Ever since that day, she had found herself growing fond of him. He was a ruthless outlaw, but he had been kind to her. LaRisa had never forgotten that. He treated her as if she were normal.

"Was it hard for Boone to accept what you can do?" LaRisa asked as she looked at her gloved hands wrapped around her teacup.

"He was a bit shocked, naturally, but he accepted it. He's come to understand my ability," Leslie told her. "My visions are part of who I am, and he loves me."

Something very close to longing stabbed through LaRisa. "Think you can have a vision to see if I'll ever find someone to love me?"

She shook her head. "A side effect of being pregnant. I can't have visions right now."

LaRisa looked at her cousin and smiled softly. "Too bad."

"You know I have no control over what I'm shown. I may never have a premonition of your future."

LaRisa opened her hands and looked at her gloved palms. "That's because I'll never have one."

Leslie reached out to touch LaRisa's palm, and she instinctively jerked her hand from her cousin's touch. "LaRisa, you're older now. You can control it. You saved my life."

LaRisa met her cousin's eyes and blinked back the sudden tears. "What if I can't touch a man with my bare hands? What if—"

"You touched Strykes," Leslie pointed out. "After we escaped the outlaws and came to your cabin, you tended his wounds. You touched him."

LaRisa nodded as she remembered the feel of his skin beneath her hands. Her cheeks heated. "I liked it."

Leslie gave her a reassuring smile. "Stop worrying. You can have a good life. A normal life, like the rest of us."

LaRisa desperately wanted to believe her cousin. "I don't know what to do."

Leslie gave her a soft smile. "Follow your heart," she said, as if it were the answer to every question in life.

"My heart?" she choked the words out as she fought not to cry. "My heart is telling me to take a chance and love him. But my head says no. It tells me to stay away from him." She turned her gloved palms up to look at them again. "I'm scared I'll hurt him. Or worse." She looked at Leslie. "I don't know what to do."

Leslie reached over and took one of LaRisa's gloved hands in both of hers. This time, she didn't jerk away. Her cousin's dark eyes filled with tears of sympathy. "I wish I could help, but this is your decision."

LaRisa nodded but couldn't speak.

"I want you to be happy. You deserve love. I believe that Strykes cares about you, and I think you should both take a chance."

"I just don't know the right choice." LaRisa brushed at her wet cheeks. Damn it, she didn't want to cry. "I don't want to hurt him, and I'm afraid he won't accept what I can do. He'll be afraid of me."

Leslie scoffed. "Nonsense. Strykes isn't afraid of anything."

LaRisa knew her cousin was right, but she herself was afraid enough for the both of them.

"Come on." Leslie stood and headed for the kitchen. "I'm hungry, and you need to be busy."

LaRisa followed Leslie into the kitchen and helped her cook lunch. She was thankful for the distraction, but all too soon, it was time to retrieve her wagon.

Bidding Leslie goodbye, she left the house. LaRisa felt better after her talk with Leslie, but she was still nervous. What if Strykes didn't want to court her? How could she encourage him? So many questions and no answers.

LaRisa pulled in a deep breath, squared her shoulders, and walked to the blacksmith's shop. Blackie was hitched to her wagon out front. She would just have to attempt to be flirtatious and see what happened.

LaRisa's heart fluttered when she saw Strykes at the bellows, heating a length of iron. Sweat glistened on his face and arms as he worked. She took a moment to enjoy watching the way his muscles moved and bunched as he worked the bellows.

"I see you have my wagon fixed," she said as she approached him. "Was it the spring?"

"Yeah." He didn't look at her, and his voice was cold.

LaRisa waited for him to elaborate, but he didn't. She studied him as he worked. His body was tense, and his mouth was a hard line. A muscle worked in his jaw, and she wasn't sure what that meant. Was he angry with her?

"Thank you," she finally said. "How much do I owe you?"

"Don't worry about it."

She frowned. "I should pay you."

"I said, don't worry about it."

"But—"

"Just go!" he snapped as he pumped the bellows.

Hurt slashed through LaRisa, and she stared at him for a moment before she turned and hurried to her wagon. Somehow seeing through the tears in her eyes, she climbed into the wagon and gathered up the reins. Fighting the urge to cry, she snapped the reins on her horse's back, and he lurched forward.

What had she done to upset Strykes? He had been so friendly to her when she had arrived. He had smiled at her. A genuine smile that made his usually cold eyes light up with something very close to happiness.

Leslie had been wrong. LaRisa never should have taken a chance and gotten her hopes up. She was never meant to have a normal life or be happy. She would never make this mistake again.

LaRisa urged her horse into a faster pace and didn't look back.

Chapter Five

Strykes stood on the hill, looking out over the town, his horse grazing happily on the green grass. He was once again thankful for the second chance he had been given.

Strykes swung up into the saddle, turned his horse, and rode away from the view of town. He wasn't sure where he was going, but he didn't care. His restless spirit was tugging at him again, and he thought a long ride would help ease his need to travel.

Years of war, drifting, and running from the law was all he had known, and it was hard for him to stay in one place for long. A new chance at a good life kept him in Rimrock. He knew Travis wouldn't throw him in jail or hang him for his past. A wry smile tugged his mouth, only because the marshal had no proof.

Suddenly, images of LaRisa filled his mind. Truth be told, she was the reason he was staying in Rimrock. Strykes once again reminded himself he needed to keep his distance from her. He had developed feelings for her, and he couldn't let those feelings grow. LaRisa would be safer that way.

Three days had passed since she had driven her wagon away from the shop. Three days since he had heard that beautiful laugh and seen the hurt in her eyes. He hadn't wanted to be cold toward her, but he had no choice.

"Damn you, Lucas," he growled.

Lucas would come after him, and he wouldn't think twice about hurting LaRisa. The cruel man would do unspeakable things to her just to add to his revenge against Strykes. Staying away from LaRisa was the only way to keep her safe.

Maybe when this was over and Lucas lay buried in the cold ground, he would beg her forgiveness.

Without warning, the report of a rifle echoed as a bullet slammed into his shoulder. The force of it nearly made him topple from the saddle, but he managed to stay seated as another bullet burned across his ribs. Wheeling the frightened horse, Strykes headed for the cover of the trees as a bullet tore through his thigh.

Ignoring the pain in his body, he focused on staying in the saddle as the mare galloped into the trees, carefully navigating the densely packed trees and fallen debris.

Strykes was now glad he had purchased the mare. She was fast, surefooted, and had stamina. She would easily outrun his ambushers. He was in no condition to fight, making running his only option.

As he rode, Strykes tried to think of the many ways he would kill Lucas and not the amount of blood he was losing. He could feel it running down his chest and soaking his thigh. His trousers were becoming saturated with his life's blood.

Strykes urged the mare on. He couldn't go back to town, knowing the man who wanted him dead would more than likely be waiting for him to head for the doctor.

He rode flat out for a couple of miles, then slowed the mare slightly. He didn't want to run her to death and have to walk. In the condition he was in, he would surely die if he were on foot. The warm flow of blood from his shoulder ran down his stomach, reminding him of just how serious his situation was. He needed help, and he needed it quick.

He frantically searched his mind as his horse loped along. There was only one place he could think of going, and that was to LaRisa's. It was several miles away, but the trail was easygoing, and his horse would make good time.

He might make it before he died. She had helped him once before. She knew her way around bullet wounds, and she was his only hope at this point.

***

LaRisa stood at her kitchen counter, filling a small jar with herbs. Mrs. Sims was running low on the tea leaves that helped ease the pain of rheumatism. Her husband had been suffering from it of late, and Sam had told the woman to come to LaRisa for more if she ran out. Though people would never admit to coming out here to get potions from the witch, it pleased LaRisa that some people were accepting her.

Sam was a well-respected doctor in Rimrock, and folks trusted his judgment. LaRisa was thankful for his help. It seemed to put people somewhat at ease when they were around her. The constant looks of fear had faded from a few faces; some were no longer afraid of her turning them into toads.

"Or sucking the life out of them," she muttered to herself.

Saber stood and growled as he stalked to the window. He stood up on his hind legs and rested his paws on the ledge. Another growl rumbled from him.

LaRisa turned from the counter and listened. The sound of a horse approaching caught her ears. It must be Mrs. Sims coming for her tea leaves. But the horse was coming in too fast.

A frown lined her face as she looked out the window at the approaching rider. Sweat streaked the horse's sides, and the man was leaning low over her neck. What the hell was going on? Who would want to see her bad enough to run their horse ragged?

She moved away from the window and lifted her rifle from its place on the wall and walked to the door. The horse had stopped in front of her house, and she took a deep breath of courage before she flung open the door and pointed the rifle at a man's chest. A broad chest, she noted, that was covered in blood. Her eyes lifted to his. She stared into a pair of pale-blue eyes that were glassy from pain.

"Mr. Strykes," she breathed in shock.

"LaRisa" was all he said before he staggered and caught himself on the door frame.

She said nothing as she set the gun aside and put his good arm around her shoulders and helped him across the room.

"Here, lay down," she said and helped him sit on the table.

He lay down with a groan of pain, his legs hanging off the edge of the table. LaRisa quickly pulled a chair around and set his feet on it to help make him more comfortable.

"What the hell happened?" she asked as she looked his bloody body over.

"I got shot," he said simply.

LaRisa made a rude noise. "I can see that."

He shifted on the table, and a groan escaped his lips. "Somebody wants me dead."

"I'd say so." Her eyes traveled his body. There was so much blood. If she didn't work fast, he would be dead soon.

When LaRisa moved to shut the door, she noticed that the bay mare was still standing in the yard, her sides heaving, head hanging. Her eyes flew to where Strykes lay on the table, his body covered with blood. She could only do so much for him; she had to get him help.

As quickly as possible, she found a pencil and paper and wrote a note: "Sam, come to my house," and signed it LR. She ran from the house and to the horse. She secured the folded paper between the saddle and saddle blanket. With any luck, it would stay there, and Roper would find it when he unsaddled the mare. That was if the horse returned to the livery.

With a whoop and a wave of her arms, LaRisa tried to scare the animal into running away. But the tired mare only pranced off a few paces before turning to look at her.

"Saber," she called for the big dog, and he appeared at her side. "Get her!" she ordered and pointed at the mare.

Saber set into a fit of barking and took after the mare. The horse sprang away at a dead run from the cabin, the dog nipping at her heels until she outran him.

When the mare had disappeared over the hill, LaRisa whistled for Saber to return. He trotted back to her, his tongue lolling happily as he panted. The mare hadn't headed toward town, but LaRisa prayed the horse would make her way back to the livery.

LaRisa rushed back into the cabin, not bothering to close the door behind her. Strykes still lay on the table, his chest rising and falling. Good—he wasn't dead.

With hurried movements, LaRisa built up the fire in the stove and placed a pan of water on it to heat. She dashed to her bedroom and grabbed a petticoat to cut into strips for bandages.

"You owe me a petticoat," she informed him.

A chuckle left him. "I'll buy you a new dress too."

"You do that."

Saber barked from the porch, and LaRisa dropped the petticoat on the floor and went to the door.

She saw the riders coming down her road, and her heart nearly stopped. There was no doubt in her mind that they were after Strykes.

Her eyes moved to the blood on her doorstep. How would she explain this to those men? A groan of dread left her as she thought frantically. Her gaze landed on the chicken coop and the hens pecking at the ground.

She stepped across the yard and quickly reached out and grabbed the chicken by the neck. It squawked and flapped its wings as she carried it to the woodpile near the cabin. In one smooth motion, she reached for the ax, set the chicken across the stump, and lopped its head off.

She grabbed the animal by the feet and hurried toward the house, pleased to note the amount of blood it was losing as she walked over the path Strykes had taken. The chicken left its own trail of blood as she entered the house, urged Saber inside, and shut the door tightly behind her.

Strykes was sitting up on the table, a hand on the bleeding wound in his shoulder. "What's going on?"

"Riders coming in fast," she told him.

He looked at the chicken in her hand. "You gonna cook them lunch?"

"No," she said simply. "I suggest you hide yourself."

Rising from the table, he limped off toward the bedroom and disappeared through the doorway. When he was gone, she tossed the chicken on the table. Its blood mingled with that of Strykes's, and she yanked out a few handfuls of feathers as she heard the riders drawing closer. Then someone was pounding on her door.

Saber growled low in his throat as LaRisa walked on unsteady legs to the door, dangling the chicken by the feet. Her eyes shot to the bedroom. The curtain that served as the door was pulled back, allowing a look into the room, and she hoped they would think she was hiding nothing.

With a breath of courage, she opened the door to see a hard-looking man covered in dust. Two more sat their horses in the yard. She opened the door fully to allow the man a look inside.

"Can I help you?" she asked calmly.

"We're part of a posse, ma'am," the short, stocky man before her said. "We're on the trail of a feller that robbed the bank in Rimrock. We lost his horse's trail, but it looked like he was heading this way. He's been shot, so we figure he's looking for someone to help him. Have you seen him?"

LaRisa eyed the men for a long moment. They didn't look like any part of a posse. She didn't know much about Strykes, other than he had ridden with a gang of outlaws for many years before coming to Rimrock. For all she knew, he had robbed the bank, but she had no doubt that the man was lying. If anyone was leading a posse, it would be Heck or Boone. If she turned

Strykes over to the men, she doubted he would make it back to town alive. If these men didn't kill him, his wounds surely would.

She nodded in answer to the man's question. "A big man on a bay horse rode in a little while ago. He tried to take my horse, so I had to run him off." She jerked her head to the rifle, leaning against the chair.

The man nodded and let out an aggravated sigh. He looked away from her and did his best not to swear. She wasn't sure whether he would slap her and call her a liar or just burst into the house and see if Strykes was there or not. When he turned back to her, his eyes saw the blood on the floor.

"What happened there?" His eyes were suspicious as he looked at the trail of blood leading into the house and to the table.

At his tone, Saber let out a low growl. She reached down and patted him on the head to put him at ease. She knew that if this man made a wrong move, her dog would tear into him. Saber was very protective, and she was once again glad her father had given him to her five years ago.

"I'm cooking," she said and held up the chicken by the feet for them to see. Blood dripped from its neck. "Would you like to stay for dinner?" she asked with a big smile, glad her voice was steady and the fear she felt didn't show. "I'd be glad for the company."

The man gave her an odd look, no doubt thinking she was a crazy woman who had lived alone too long. "No thanks, ma'am. We'd better be getting along. Which way did he go?"

She used the hand holding the chicken to point. "Up over the hill there," she said, gesturing in the direction opposite the one the bay mare had gone in.

"Thanks," he muttered as he turned. He didn't give her a backward glance as he walked back to his horse and mounted up.

She didn't close the door until all three riders were out of sight. Then she turned and staggered back to the table on suddenly weak legs. She tossed the chicken on the top and let out a shuddering sigh.

"Good job," Strykes said from behind her.

She gave a start and turned to see him standing in the doorway, his pistol in hand. "It was the only thing I could think of."

He nodded his appreciation and took two limping steps toward her before he fell to the floor. She was at his side in an instant. He was out cold.

What should she do now? She wished Sam were here. She had dressed Strykes's wounds before when he had been shot, but they hadn't been this bad.

Working quickly, she washed up and grabbed a knife before picking up her petticoat. She frantically cut it into strips. When she finished, she dashed to the stove to remove the now-hot water, then knelt on the floor next to him.

She took his pistol from his hand. Even passed out, he clung tightly to it. She slid the gun away before she removed his gun belt.

As carefully as she could, she began cutting away his blood-soaked shirt. With that done, she turned her attention to his trousers, and a reluctant groan escaped her lips as she began slicing through the material. She grabbed a blanket from her bed, and her heart hammered as she removed his trousers and then laid the blanket over his narrow hips. She couldn't keep her eyes from straying or her cheeks from blushing.

When she had finished shedding him of all his clothing, she surveyed the damage. He had been shot to hell. A hole went through his thigh. Another bullet was in his right shoulder. A third had torn a groove across his left side, and he had been grazed on the upper part of his left arm.

"I'd say someone wanted you dead pretty bad," she whispered as she washed the wounds. "What kind of trouble are you in this time?"

LaRisa's anxiety grew as she did what she could for Strykes. The bullet was still in his shoulder, and his thigh was still bleeding freely. Tears burned her eyes as she looked at his pale face. He was going to die this time. Her hands shook as she paused to look at his wounds. Could she save him?

"I can't," she whimpered as she balled her hands into fists.

She blinked back her tears and knew she had no choice. If she didn't try, Strykes would die, but even if she did this, he might still die. She didn't want to be responsible for his death. She didn't want to kill the only person outside her family who wasn't afraid of her.

Taking a deep breath of courage, LaRisa moved her hands over the holes in his thigh. She had to stop the bleeding; she would have to heal the wound. Her heart pounded with fear as she closed her eyes and did her best to focus on the energy.

"Please, God, don't let me kill him," she prayed as she let the energy flow.

The heat in her hands was intense as she held them over the wounds in his thigh. After a few moments, the energy slowed, and the heat lessened. She took a deep breath and pulled her hands away from him. The wound was gone; only the blood smeared on his thigh was evidence it had once been there.

LaRisa sat up, and her head spun as black spots gathered behind her eyes. She noticed Strykes was still breathing as the blackness overtook her and she slumped over onto the floor.

Chapter Six

Strykes came awake slowly and was instantly aware of the pain radiating through his body. He clenched his teeth against a groan as he tried to remember what the hell had happened to him. Everything was a haze as he forced himself to think, and the realization he had been ambushed went through his mind. They had shot him.

"Strykes?"

The soft feminine voice pulled him fully awake, and he managed to get his eyes to open. He had to blink several times to get them to focus on the woman who was leaning over him. He lay on the floor, covered with blankets, and LaRisa was there with him. She sat beside him, watching him intently with those beautiful emerald eyes.

"LaRisa," he said, though his voice was rough.

"I'm glad you're awake," she said with relief, but her body was still tense, and concern lined her features. She dabbed at his forehead with a cool rag. "I was worried about you."

He couldn't keep his eyes from closing. He was exhausted. "How long was I out?"

"A couple hours," she said and continued to wash his face.

There was a tone to her voice that made him force his eyes open again. "What is it?"

She sighed and set the rag aside to place a hand on his chest, absently brushing her fingers over the coarse hair as she chewed her lower lip. "Strykes, the bullet is still in your shoulder."

"Then you'll have to dig it out," he told her calmly.

She looked from the bloody hole in his shoulder to his eyes. "I don't know if I can do it."

"You have to."

She swallowed hard. "W-what if I kill you?"

"If you don't take it out, I'll die anyway," he explained to her softly.

She stared at him. "How can you be so casual about this?"

He gave a small shrug and swore at the pain it caused. "That's just how it is, LaRisa. Getting upset over things won't help me any."

Her eyes moved to his shoulder again. "I put a note under your saddle. I told Sam to come here."

"There isn't time to wait for him." He placed a hand over hers. "You have to do it."

She looked at him with those eyes, and he was lost. Her beautiful face was filled with fear, her eyes full of pain. He wanted to take her in his arms and tell her that everything would be fine and that she could do this. He just might have if it didn't hurt so damn much to move.

"LaRisa?"

She swallowed hard. "I'll try," she told him and placed her other hand over the top of his and gave it a light squeeze. "I just want to tell you that if I end up killing you, I'm sorry." She blinked, and tears slipped free.

"LaRisa, come here," he whispered.

She leaned closer to hear him better. His hand came up and grabbed the back of her neck. He pulled her down until their lips met. Her lips were soft and her mouth sweet. A perfect kiss from a perfect woman before he died.

LaRisa didn't know what to do. She knew she shouldn't let him, but she was afraid if she pushed him away, she might hurt him further. But she didn't want to push him away. His lips were gentle on hers, and she felt her stomach muscles tighten from the sensation. Then his hand fell away, and he lay back, unconscious.

LaRisa sat back and stared at him with tearful eyes, her fingers splayed across her lips. How in the hell was she supposed to function now? Her nerves were already a mess, and now that he had kissed her, she didn't know what to do. She had to calm down and get a hold of herself if she was going to save his life.

LaRisa pulled in a deep breath and let it out slowly as she tried to think of the best way to help Strykes. Her eyes went to the hole in his shoulder, and she knew she didn't have the right tools to properly get the bullet out. She would probably do more damage than good.

"I don't want to do this," she whimpered even as she got to her feet and gathered what she thought she might need.

With shaking hands, LaRisa poured fresh water, gathered bandages, and picked up a long, slender knife. She looked at the knife for a long moment and hoped that she could get the bullet out with it. Images of slicing through his shoulder and damaging him further went through her mind.

"Stop it," she ordered herself as she shook the thoughts off.

Before her mind could wander again and she lost her nerve, she knelt beside Strykes and placed her items on the floor within easy reach. She cast a nervous look at Saber, who lay near the door, watching her intently. She knew he couldn't help her, but having him near made her feel a little better.

She lifted the knife and swallowed hard as she looked at the wound in Strykes's shoulder. "This is probably gonna hurt," she told the unconscious man.

She hoped she could get this done before he came to. She was sure he would come up fighting, and she didn't want to be on the receiving end of it.

Forcing her shaking hands to be steady, LaRisa used the knife to probe the wound. Blood oozed up around the blade. After a moment, she felt the point come into contact with something hard. Now what?

With no other choice, she used the blade to force the bullet to come out. Though she tried to be gentle, she knew she was causing damage to his body.

She let out a small cry of relief when she pulled the bullet free. Blood poured from the wound, and her relief was replaced with panic.

"No, no, no!" She frantically placed a bandage over the wound, and it was soaked through in seconds. "No, this can't happen!"

Without thinking, LaRisa pulled the bandage away and slapped her palm to the wound, sending her healing energy into Strykes. Fighting down panic, she watched the blood ooze from around her hand, and she knew he was going to die. Tears filled her eyes and spilled down her cheeks as she fought for control.

"Don't die," she begged as she pushed her energy deeper.

The blood flow slowed, and relief almost touched her when she felt the energy inside her shift. Instead of giving, her body began to take. Her panic intensified as Strykes groaned and moved restlessly, as if he knew something was going horribly wrong.

With a cry, LaRisa snatched her hand from his shoulder and scrambled several feet away from him. Her body trembled violently, and she fought against the waves of nausea and the need to faint.

Saber was at her side in an instant, and she clung to her dog desperately as she forced her eyes to focus on Strykes. Her vision was hazy, but she could see that he was still breathing, and the blood coming from his shoulder was only a trickle.

"Thank God," she breathed and buried her face in Saber's fur as she fought against the warring energies within her body.

LaRisa swallowed hard against the need to vomit, yet another side effect of what she could do. Of what she had almost done. She took a few moments to get herself under control as she hugged her dog tightly. She couldn't give in to the need to be sick or faint. Strykes still needed her, and she would not let him down.

Reluctantly, LaRisa released Saber and turned to look at Strykes. He still lay there on the floor, pale as death, but his breathing was steady, though shallow. She needed to clean and bandage the wound to stop the remaining bleeding.

Blinking back the fogginess in her eyes and pushing away the gathering blackness that tried to take her, she moved to kneel beside Strykes. Forcing herself to control her shaking, she cleaned and dressed the wound in his shoulder.

She had healed the wound enough to stop the severe bleeding and keep infection from setting in. He would still have a serious wound but would have no idea that she had healed the majority of it.

"My secret is still safe," she whispered as she finished bandaging the man's shoulder.

LaRisa pulled the blankets up over Strykes and hoped he would stay warm sleeping on the floor. Tomorrow she would make sure he was more comfortable, but this was going to have to do for now.

With an exhausted groan, LaRisa moved away from him to lie on the floor close by. She gave in to the gathering blackness behind her eyes and passed out.

Saber walked to her and sat next to her to watch over her as the warring energies inside her fought.

***

LaRisa slowly came awake as she heard Saber let out a low growl from beside her. She lifted her head and sat up as she rubbed at her eyes, trying to get them to focus. She instantly looked at Strykes, and for a moment, fear gripped her, but she saw the small rise and fall of his chest as he breathed.

She moved to kneel beside him, her body aching after sleeping on the hard floor, and placed a hand on his forehead and was relieved that he wasn't feverish. "You just might make it," she told him as she stroked a hand down his whiskered jaw.

Another growl from Saber brought her attention around. He was on his feet, walking toward the window. He hopped up on his hind legs, his front paws on the window ledge, and stared out into the yard.

She stood and walked to the window. "What is it?"

With a yawn, she peeked out the window to see what had caught Saber's attention. She didn't have to wait long before a rider rounded the bend, his horse at an easy lope. Her heart pounded, and she was about ready to dash for the rifle when she recognized the rider.

"Sam." A wave of relief washed over her as she rushed to the door to fling it open and watch him approach. Saber went out to greet him, barking and wagging his tail.

He pulled his horse to a halt in front of her and easily swung down. She watched him tie his horse to the small tree in her yard before he removed his black bag from the back of the saddle. He said nothing, but she didn't miss the way his dark eyes scanned the hills around her cabin.

"Sam, I'm glad you're here," she told him as he walked up to her. "Strykes is here, and he's in bad shape."

"Strykes is here?" he asked, but he didn't wait for an answer as LaRisa stepped aside to allow him and the dog to enter before she closed the door.

"He rode in yesterday, he's been shot," she told him quickly.

Sam's eyes moved around the room, and they lit on Strykes lying on the floor. He instantly moved to the man's side and checked over the damage.

"Christ, what happened?"

"I'm not sure. Someone shot him."

Sam nodded. "How has Strykes been?"

"He's been out for hours. I did everything I could for him," LaRisa explained, standing over Sam's shoulder as he leaned over Strykes.

"You did good," Sam told her as he checked the wounds.

"I did my best," she said self-consciously.

"Did you try to heal him?"

She swallowed hard. "I healed his leg. I couldn't get the bleeding to stop. It was the only thing I could think of to save him. I had to dig the bullet out of his shoulder, and I was sure he was going to die." Tears filled her eyes, and she blinked them back as she looked at Strykes lying pale as death on the floor. "I tried to heal it, but then the energy changed…" She hugged herself and tried not to think of what she could have done. "At least I haven't killed him yet."

Sam slowly met her eyes. "Nobody blames you for what happened back then," he told her gently.

The old familiar pain went through her as she tried not to think about that day so many years ago. "I do."

"LaRisa, we've gone over this. It wasn't your fault. You were scared and too young to control it."

"Is he going to live?" she asked before they got into the same old argument.

He nodded and went along with her change of subject. "As long as no infection sets in, I think he's got a good chance of pulling through. He's lost a lot of blood, and it will be some time before he regains his strength."

"Some men stopped here looking for him, and I lied and sent them on their way. I don't think they believed me," she quickly explained.

Sam stood with his black bag in hand and met her eyes. "They didn't. I thought I saw riders in the hills when I rode up. It looks like they're watching your place."

LaRisa felt her heart pound with fear. "What should I do? Strykes won't be able to leave here any time soon."

"I'll tell Boone and Heck we think you're being watched," Sam told her. "I'm sure they'll send someone out to keep an eye on you."

LaRisa nodded absently, though it only slightly put her at ease. Knowing a bunch of evil men were watching her cabin scared the hell out of her, but she would feel better if there was also someone out there she trusted to watch them.

"But you be careful, LaRisa," Sam told her, unable to hide the worry in his voice. "Whoever is after Strykes isn't messing around. They want him dead mighty bad."

LaRisa swallowed hard and nodded as a fresh wave of fear washed over her. "I'll be careful."

"And keep him out of sight until he's strong enough to leave. Maybe by then Heck and Boone will have whoever is out there run off or in jail."

"Okay." Fear gnawed at her stomach, and she fought it down with an effort.

"Gather me some herbs to take back with me. If someone is watching, I want them to think I came here for herbs."

LaRisa nodded and quickly went to her little cabinet in the kitchen, where she kept her herbs. Her hands shook as she gathered the small cloth bags of various dried herbs and placed them in a canvas bag. She knew Sam was right. If anyone was watching, it would be better if they thought he had come on business.

After tying the bag shut, she turned and handed it to Sam. "I think you were running low on some of these anyway."

"Perfect." He held the bag easily in his big hand. "Keep your gun handy, and don't take any chances."

"I'll be careful. Strykes needs clothes. If you could send True or my mother out with some, I'd appreciate it," she told him and felt her cheeks heat at the thought of seeing Strykes naked.

"I will." He headed for the door, and LaRisa followed him outside to his horse. "I'll be honest and tell you I don't like the thought of him here alone with you."

"I understand, but I'll be fine," she assured him.

"I'll send someone out tomorrow with clothes for him."

"Thank you, Sam."

He nodded and mounted his horse to ride out at an easy pace. She watched him leave and couldn't keep her eyes from scanning the hills beyond the cabin. Someone was out there watching her and just waiting for any evidence that Strykes was, in fact, with her. She had to make sure he stayed inside and didn't let anyone see him.

Once he was well enough, they would think of a way to get him to town, where he would be safer. The safest way would be to go through the caves. Nobody would see them or be able to follow them. LaRisa knew the caves well, and she could guide them to safety.

Until then, she would have to go about her daily routine as if nothing was wrong. She would have to act as though she wasn't hiding a wounded man in her cabin, and she hoped she would be convincing.

Heaving a deep sigh, LaRisa turned and went back into her cabin. She closed and bolted the door, then leaned against it for a moment as she collected her nerves. She had isolated herself in her cabin to keep away from people and the trouble that came with them. She turned to look at Strykes as he lay on the cabin floor. He was bringing trouble to her life again.

LaRisa walked to him and sat on the floor, watching the man sleep, and thought of their acquaintance. She hardly knew him, yet he had affected her life in so many ways. She had saved his life twice. He was the first man to treat her like a human and the first man to innocently touch her, to dance with her, and he had kissed her.

LaRisa thought back to when she had first patched up his wounds. He had been shot after helping Leslie escape from an outlaw gang. A gang he had been a part of. LaRisa had been bandaging him when he reached out and touched her hair. He pulled the ribbon free and let her auburn locks fill his hands as if savoring the softness.

Then he had touched her face. It had been just a light brush, but it had set her heart racing. He had touched her with such tender fascination, and it caused feelings in her she had never known existed. His hand was big and calloused, but he had been so gentle when he touched her.

She remembered him the day of Leslie and Boone's wedding. She had made an appearance and was about to make her way through the crowd and head for home when Strykes had stopped her. He had asked her to dance. Before she could even answer, he took her in his arms and whisked her around the dance floor. She remembered how nice it felt to be in his arms and to be treated like a human.

Now, here he was again, shot up in her cabin. This time, he had kissed her. She wished he hadn't passed out. She had never been kissed before and it had been very startling, yet there had also been something there she didn't understand. A feeling she couldn't quite grasp. A feeling she wanted to explore.

Chapter Seven

Strykes drifted through the fog of sleep. His body hurt, and he didn't know why. Had he taken another beating? Though he tried to wake up, he couldn't. Had his father knocked him out again? One day, the beatings would stop.

His thoughts drifted, and he found himself standing on the porch of their small house on the plantation. He couldn't be here. He hadn't been here since the war started. Why was he here now?

The anguished scream echoed in the air, and Strykes ran for the barn. It was Willow. The screaming continued, and he ran faster. He had to help his sister. He had to stop what was about to happen.

Strykes ran into the barn to see his father and Willow. She was on the ground with him over her, his hands around her throat. Her eyes were wide with fear, her breath coming in strangled gasps.

With a howl of rage, Strykes lunged for the man. He jerked his father from Willow, and she lay there gasping for air. Blind with rage, Strykes delivered blow after blow to the man's body. His father tried in vain to defend himself, but he was no match for Strykes's greater strength.

Willow shouted a warning, but it was too late. Strykes felt the searing pain in his side the instant he heard the gunshot. Strykes delivered another solid blow to his father's face. The man spun and went to his knees. Strykes dropped behind him, and in one swift motion, he broke the man's neck. He crumpled to the ground, the pistol still in his hand.

The beatings would stop now. But he was too late to help his little sister. He was always too late.

He rushed to where Willow lay crumpled on the ground. He dropped to his knees and rolled her into his arms. She was breathing, her face bruised and her lips cut. He lifted her to him, and she cried out. He laid her back and quickly looked her over for any damage. There was blood on her dress, and her right leg lay at an awkward angle, and he knew it was broken. He lifted her dress to look at her leg and swore loudly. The bone had broken through the skin, and he had to swallow back the bile that rose.

He looked to where his father lay. The man would never hurt his family again. But the damage he had caused was something that could never be changed. Lives couldn't be given back.

Strykes slowly came awake at the sound of soft singing. He lay there for a long time, listening to the beautiful voice. When he had the energy, Strykes rolled open his eyes to see the morning sun drift into the cabin. Where the hell was he? He wasn't at the plantation, and he wasn't in the barn. It wasn't his little sister's voice that he heard.

He blinked several times and did his best to focus. He was in a cabin, LaRisa's cabin. His mind then registered the pain in his body. He hadn't taken a beating. He had been shot and had come to LaRisa for help.

Strykes managed to turn his head toward the beautiful voice, and he saw LaRisa moving around the kitchen as she sang the haunting melody. Damn, he could listen to her for hours. Her voice slid over him like a caress. He had heard nothing so beautiful in his life. His eyes closed, and he listened to her as he hung on the edge of sleep.

Strykes fought to stay conscious. He wanted to hear LaRisa sing. Her voice was beautiful. He never knew she possessed such a talent and was secretly pleased that she was sharing it with him. Even if she didn't know it.

The image of LaRisa singing to a child in her arms went through his mind. A child with black hair and pale-blue eyes. His child.

"No," he muttered and shook off the image. "It can't happen."

LaRisa's singing abruptly stopped. "Strykes?"

"You'll hurt her," he whispered to himself as he tried to shake away the images. "You'll hurt them both."

"Strykes."

Her voice was close, and he felt her hands on his face. Her hands were soft and warm, instantly calming him in a way he didn't understand.

"Strykes, it's all right," she soothed. "Nobody is hurting anybody."

Her hand brushed across his forehead, and Strykes felt himself relax. A kind of peace washed over him at her touch, and he wished she would touch him forever. A wish that would never be reality.

"Can you open your eyes?" she asked gently.

Strykes fought to pry his eyes open, but they refused to obey him. He wanted to see LaRisa, wanted to see her beautiful face and forget he was on the threshold of death. He tried to lift his hand to touch her, but pain radiated across his shoulder, and he groaned through clenched teeth.

"Don't move," she ordered gently. "You need to save your strength. You've lost a lot of blood and will be weak for a while."

Strykes wanted to swear in frustration but didn't have the energy. He felt weak and helpless—a feeling that did not set well with him. He hadn't been weak or helpless since he was a boy. And he had made a vow to never be that way again.

****

When Strykes could pull himself awake, he looked up at the ceiling. Judging from the sun coming through the windows, it was dawn. How long had he been out this time?

He blinked the remaining haze from his eyes and looked around. His breath caught when he saw LaRisa. She lay on her side next to him. He allowed himself the luxury of watching her for a while. Her face was relaxed in sleep, her long lashes resting against cheeks that had a light dusting of freckles on them. Her auburn hair was in a loose braid that lay across her neck. Several strands had escaped and settled across her cheek and forehead. He could never get over just how beautiful she was.

His eyes traveled down her slender neck, over her shoulder, and down her arm. Her hand rested curled up near her lips. Lips, he noted, that were full and slightly parted, perfect for kissing. Lips that he had kissed, and they had been perfect. He smiled slightly to himself and let his gaze go lower. Her full breasts strained against the front of her dress, and the two top buttons were undone, allowing him a look that made his body ache with need.

He frowned when his eyes reached her waist. Two dark brown paws hung there. He followed the paws until he reached the even darker brown eyes of Saber. The big dog was draped protectively over her waist, his chin resting in the curve, his eyes watching Strykes's every move. For a moment, Strykes envied the dog and resented him. As if knowing this, Saber curled his lips and growled softly.

LaRisa stirred at the sound and blinked her eyes open. She immediately looked at Strykes, and when she saw his eyes looking back, she smiled. He couldn't have moved or have said anything if he wanted to. Her smile had frozen him in place. It was such a sweet, truly blissful smile that made her eyes dance. Eyes that had always seemed so empty and haunted were now alive and happy. And she was absolutely beautiful.

"Good morning," she whispered in a sleepy voice.

He favored her with a slight smile of his own. "I could get used to waking up like this." His voice was rough; he told himself it was because he had slept so long, and he was thirsty.

"Like how?" she asked, propping herself up on one elbow. Her movement disturbed Saber, and he sat up, still watching Strykes.

"Waking up next to such a beautiful woman every morning." He saw her blush, and she lowered her eyes, but her smile brightened. "Glad you didn't kill me. It gave me the chance to enjoy such an event."

When she looked at him again, her smile was gone and the sparkle in her eyes had vanished. "I need to check your bandages," she said hollowly and stood.

He closed his eyes again, suddenly feeling tired. He heard the door open for Saber to go out and was almost glad the dog was gone. The dog took his role of protecting her to the extreme. If LaRisa ever married, her husband would have to fight the dog just to get into the marriage bed with her.

He opened his eyes when he heard her approaching him. She carried a pan of water and clean bandages. Her face was expressionless as she began removing the bandage on his shoulder to wash the wound. He could feel a tension he didn't understand radiating from her, and it worried him. Maybe she was upset at what he had said.

"I'm sorry if I made you angry," Strykes said in way of an apology. It was strange how a woman could make a man do things he hadn't done before. He had never apologized to anyone in his life before, yet he had seen her reaction to his words and wanted to put her at ease. Mostly, he wanted the sparkle back in her eyes. "I wasn't implying that you'd kill me on purpose or anything."

She didn't look at him, only kept her eyes on the task of bandaging his shoulder up again. "No, I wouldn't kill you on purpose."

"Thank you for helping me."

"I didn't have much choice," she said simply. "You were hurt, and I couldn't very well turn you away." She stilled a moment and met his eyes. "Why did you come here?"

"I was bleeding out, and your place was the closest. You helped me once before," he told her honestly. "All I could think of was getting here to you and hoping you'd help me again."

She nodded and went back to bandaging his shoulder. "You better eat something while you're awake."

"I would love some food. I'm starving."

She finished tying off the bandage and sat back. "It won't take me long to heat something for you."

He watched her stand and gather the soiled bandages and the pan of water. She set them on the table before going to the stove and set a pot of coffee to heat before placing another pot he assumed had food in it on the stovetop.

Strykes shifted his position on the floor and felt pain move through him. It wasn't the first time he had been shot, but it was certainly the worst. He couldn't stop the groan that escaped him as he tried to sit up. He hurt like hell. His head spun, and he lay back down.

"Be careful," LaRisa scolded. "You'll tear your shoulder open."

"Yes, dear," he drawled.

She shot him a scowl before she disappeared into her bedroom and returned shortly with pillows and blankets. "I'll help you sit up."

Strykes tried to sit up again, and with LaRisa's help, he did so. She propped the pillows and blankets behind him. She placed a hand on his good shoulder and eased him back into the softness of the pillows. It felt good to sit up, but her hands on his bare skin felt even better.

Strykes went rigid. With his good arm, he lifted the blanket and looked down at himself. He was naked. He dropped the blanket back to cover himself.

LaRisa fluffed the pillow behind him a bit more. "There you go. That should be more comfortable." She knelt beside him again, and her attention went to his bandaged shoulder, making sure he wasn't bleeding.

"LaRisa?"

"What?" she met his eyes. "Does it hurt to sit up?"

"No."

"What is it?" Her eyes were full of concern.

"Where are my clothes?" He fought back a smile when he saw her cheeks flush, and she looked away.

"Th-they were all bloody," she stammered and focused on his shoulder. "I had to take them off."

"You?" A chuckle rumbled in his chest. "You undressed me?"

"I couldn't let you lay there in bloody clothes," she informed him, daring a glance at him.

"I sure wish I had been awake for that." He favored her with a small smile. "Think I might have enjoyed it."

She frowned at him. "If you had been awake, I wouldn't have had to undress you. You could have done it yourself."

He gave her his best shocked look. "In my condition? I'm not sure I could have managed." He leaned closer to her; his shoulder protested, but he didn't care. "I'm sure I would have needed your help. Might have been fun."

LaRisa stared at him in shock. "What is wrong with you?"

"I'm a man, LaRisa. Having a beautiful woman undress me is a very nice thought."

"Well, stop thinking like that. It was something that had to be done."

"Wish I would have been awake for the bath too," he drawled.

Her face heated even more. "I couldn't very well leave you all bloody."

"You're right." Strykes grew serious and nodded. "I'm sorry."

She nodded and tugged the bandage back into place. "Now you are finally talking sense."

"We'll just have to try it again when I'm not all shot up and passed out." His voice was low.

Her eyes were wide when they met his. His pale eyes held hers steadily. The teasing was gone. He was dead serious. She swallowed hard and quickly got to her feet to hurry to the stove and the pot of food.

Strykes watched her as she stirred the contents of the pot before getting a tin cup hanging from a nail on the wall near the stove. She poured coffee into the cup and turned to walk back to him.

"Here," she said and held the cup out to him.

Strykes lifted his good arm and took it from her. "Thanks."

"Sam said he'd send someone out with clothes," she said, her voice betraying the nervous tension she felt. "Your clothes were ruined."

"I can imagine," he grumbled as he sipped the coffee. It was good. "Probably full of holes and covered with blood."

"They were."

He lifted his eyes to watch her walk back to the stove and stir the contents of the pot once again. His mind focused on his body to assess the damage. His shoulder hurt like hell, and there was a small bandage on the opposite arm. He looked to see another on his side. He had been hurt a little more than he had thought. Strykes flexed one thigh muscle at a time and waited for pain. There was none, only soreness in his left thigh.

Strykes frowned as he set the cup aside, and his hand went to his thigh. There was no bandage. He was sure he had been shot in the leg. Of course, it had all happened so fast he couldn't be sure. On the ride to her cabin, he had been focused on not passing out, not counting the holes in his body.

A frown creased his brow. He had been ambushed. Lucas. It had to be Lucas, come to get his revenge on Strykes for killing Fisher. He knew the man well, and he wouldn't give up on killing Strykes until Lucas stood over his dead body.

"Where is my gun?" he asked her as he looked around the cabin. He saw it hanging over the back of the kitchen chair. "Can you bring it here?"

She turned from the stove and frowned at him. "I don't think you need it. I'll help you; you don't have to hold me at gunpoint."

He gave her a slight smile. "I don't intend to. I just feel better with it close."

She shrugged, moved to get the holster from the back of the chair, and handed it to him. He took it and carefully checked it over, then after it passed his inspection, he placed it beside him.

She went back to the stove and filled a bowl of stew for him. She walked to him and knelt.

"Here. Eat as much as you can while you're awake."

Strykes did his best to balance the bowl on his thigh, steadying it with his right hand and using his left to hold the spoon. He muttered a curse as he spilled a bit of stew. He could shoot a pistol accurately with both hands but couldn't handle a spoon.

He took a bite and savored the flavor. "Mmm. Chicken stew."

She nodded and stood. "That chicken saved your life."

He wouldn't disagree with her about that. Her quick thinking had saved him, and he would forever be grateful.

He did his best to focus on eating, but he couldn't keep from watching her. She busied herself around the kitchen placing the soiled bandages in boiling water to clean. A smile tugged his mouth.

"Next time you're in town, order yourself a new dress and petticoat."

She turned to look at him, puzzled until she remembered her comment to him about owing her a new petticoat. "I'll do that."

She gave him a bright smile before she turned back to the boiling pot to stir the bandages around. Damn, she was beautiful. Strykes figured getting shot was worth it. He got to spend time with LaRisa.

After his second bowl of stew, Strykes felt exhausted. He fought it for as long as he could but lost. He set aside the bowl and settled back into the pillows and blankets.

He was aware of LaRisa covering him and touching his forehead to check for fever. He felt quite content as sleep took him.

Chapter Eight

LaRisa was out tending to her garden when Saber barked. She looked down the road to see a buggy coming. She smiled when she recognized it. The single passenger was her aunt True.

Brushing the dirt from her dress, she walked to meet her aunt in the yard as she pulled her buggy to a stop. "Good morning," she greeted.

True smiled at her. "Morning. I'm on my way to visit your mother and brought a few things for Strykes."

She reached for the cloth bundle on the seat beside her and handed it to LaRisa. Strykes would be very glad to have clothes—though she would miss looking at his muscular chest.

"How is he doing?" True inquired.

"Better. He sleeps all the time, but there is no infection."

"Sleep is probably the best thing for him. I'll let Sam know he's doing better."

"Thank you for bringing him clothes." She felt her cheeks heat at the thought of her aunt knowing she had a naked man in her house.

True smiled down at her from her carriage seat. "If you need anything else, just let us know."

"Thank you, True," LaRisa said gratefully as she held the bundle in her arms.

She stood there watching until the carriage had rounded the bend and disappeared into the trees. Letting out a sigh, she headed back to the house, her thoughts a million miles away.

At least she could count on her family when she needed help. She might have never had any friends and people might always fear her, but she would always have her family.

She opened the door, stepped into the cabin, and shut the door quietly behind her, not wanting to disturb Strykes as he slept.

When she turned, she found herself looking into the business end of Strykes's pistol. She let out a startled cry and dropped the bundle on the floor. He was seated on his makeshift bed, propped up with one arm, his face pale, but the hand holding the pistol was steady.

His eyes focused on her, and he immediately lowered the gun. "I'm sorry. Reflexes." He placed the gun on the floor beside him and dragged a hand over his face. "Who else is here? I heard a wagon."

"It was my aunt True," she explained. "She brought some clothes for you." She indicated to the bundle at her feet.

His eyes flickered to the floor to see something wrapped in cloth. "Why are they wrapped up?" he asked, as if he didn't believe her.

The fear of seeing the gun pointed at her gave way to irritation, and she stooped to pick up the clothing. "How do you think it would have looked if someone saw her bring me men's clothing? If someone is watching, they would've been a little curious about that." She gave him a cynical look. "Don't ya think?"

Strykes watched as she ripped open the bundle and uncovered two pairs of trousers, a dark-green shirt, and a blue checked shirt. She held them up for him to inspect, then threw them into the nearest chair with a move that told him she was annoyed with him. He felt bad about pulling his gun on her, but he had been awake for all of thirty seconds and had no idea what was happening.

"Sorry about that," he said and lay back down. All his energy had been used for the simple task of sitting up. "I didn't mean to scare you."

"It's understandable. For all you knew I was coming to kill you," she said as she moved to the stove and dipped stew into a bowl. "I want you to eat before you go passing out on me again," she told him and moved across the room to him.

It was only then that he realized he was starving. The scent of the stew set his mouth watering, and his stomach rumbled.

She knelt next to him and set the bowl down, then she reached out and helped him sit up. He found it amazing that his body didn't hurt nearly as badly as he had thought it would. He was short on strength, but other than that, he felt surprisingly well. She propped pillows and blankets behind him to help support him. Then she handed him the bowl.

"Thanks," he muttered and began spooning the nourishing stew into his mouth. "True didn't happen to pack my makings, did she?"

LaRisa shook her head. "No, she didn't."

"Damn," Strykes muttered. "I could sure use a good smoke right now."

"I'll not have you stinking up my cabin, thank you very much," LaRisa informed him as she went back to the stove and dished out her own bowl of stew. "She sent a razor for you."

He absently brushed the back of his hand along his jaw to feel the growth of his whiskers. "Good thing. If I go much longer, I'll start to look like a mountain man."

LaRisa sat at the table and ate. Strykes watched her as he ate. She was such a beautiful woman, and he often wondered why she wasn't married. Sometimes she seemed a bit skittish, but she had a side to her he found irresistible. His eyes focused on her mouth, and he remembered the brief kiss he had given her.

"Are you mad at me for kissing you?" he asked without thinking.

Her eyes snapped up to look at him and her mouth opened, but no words came out. She cleared her throat and tried again. "No," she told him, and her cheeks colored slightly before she focused on her bowl of stew again. "Wh-why did you do it?"

He gave a shrug; it caused a rush of pain to go through him and he winced. "I figured I was as good as dead, so why not?"

"Thanks a lot," she snapped as she gave him a hard look, unable to hide the irritation in her voice. "It's so nice to know that only a dying man would want to kiss me."

Strykes almost wanted to laugh at her reaction but didn't think it would be a good idea. "LaRisa, I didn't mean that the way it sounded." He placed his now-empty bowl on the floor beside him.

She got to her feet and stomped toward him, grabbed his bowl, took it to the stove, and quickly scooped out a bowl full of stew for him. Taking a breath to calm herself, she turned and walked toward him. He looked up at her with those clear eyes, and she could see the smirk waiting in ambush behind his mustache. For a moment, she thought of dumping the bowl of stew out on his head.

"Here," she said as she handed it out to him.

He took the warm bowl in his large hands. "LaRisa, I didn't mean to—"

"Put some food in your mouth so it's occupied. That way you won't insult me for a while." She spun on her heel and headed for the door. "I have a garden to tend to."

Strykes watched her as she marched for the door. "Would it help if I said I *wanted* to kiss you, and I've wanted to kiss you for a long time?"

She paused in the act of opening the door, half turned toward him, then straightened her shoulders and continued outside.

When the door was shut tightly, she stopped and took a deep breath. A smile crept over her lips, and she headed for her little garden.

***

When LaRisa entered the house after watering her garden, she was startled to see Strykes up and dressed. He stood before her small mirror and washstand, face lathered and a razor in his hand.

"Damn it," he swore.

LaRisa glared at him, then smiled. He was holding the razor awkwardly and trying to shave. He wasn't having much luck, and she could see where he had nicked his neck. His eyes moved to her, and he quirked a brow.

"You gonna stand there and laugh while I cut my head off?" he asked, a bit irritated.

"Please, don't cut your head off," she said as she approached him. "I don't want to have to clean another of your bloody messes."

He glowered at her. "Your compassion astounds me."

She smiled and took the razor from him. "Go sit down, and I'll help you." She grabbed a towel and the water basin and went to the table.

Strykes sat in the kitchen chair, patiently waiting for her. "This is humiliating," he grumbled.

She took his chin in her hand and tipped his head back. "Why's that?" she asked as she brought the razor down along his cheek.

"Having to have someone else shave me makes me feel like an invalid," he groused, though he enjoyed the feel of her hands on his face.

She smiled at him. "Strykes, you were shot. I'm sure your shoulder still hurts like the blazes."

"I'm sure it could hurt all the time if I get treatment like this." He smiled back, his pale eyes twinkling.

She shook her head and wiped the razor on the towel before she continued. "Well, considering you barged into my cabin, all shot up, and I had to patch you up. You've been living here, eating my food, taking up my space, irritating me, and are generally being a pain." She gave him a teasing smile. "I guess shaving you is the least I can do for you."

A laugh rumbled in his chest as he clasped his hands together in his lap. The need to reach for her and pull her close was strong. "You're so kind."

She stepped into him and lifted his chin to run the razor up his neck. "Don't get used to it. One of these days you might manage to keep from getting shot and do this yourself."

"I don't know. It seems worth getting shot if I can get you to take care of me."

She shook her head and said nothing as she continued to shave him. She left his mustache, thick and black as it ran along his mouth, almost to his chin in a horseshoe fashion. It was a style she liked on him. She laid down the razor and picked up her scissors to trim the mustache back. She looked at it for a long moment before she lowered her mouth to his.

Strykes watched in shocked pleasure as she lowered her head and brushed her mouth over his. Fire settled in his stomach, and his hands clenched until his knuckles turned white. She captured his lips fully and tipped his head back to tease her mouth over his. Jesus, he wanted this woman, and he knew full well he couldn't have her.

She pulled back and ran her thumb over his mouth. "Perfect." Her thumb trailed over the side of his mustache to his chin. "It doesn't tickle anymore."

She straightened and wiped the rest of the lather from his face. Her heart hammered, her eyes went wide, and her face heated as what she had just done registered. She had kissed him! What in the world had possessed her to do that? She was shocked, and he looked extremely pleased.

"I'm finished," she said quickly and turned from him.

Strykes muttered a curse as she moved away from him and began cleaning up. It took every ounce of control he could muster to keep from grabbing her and dragging her into her bedroom.

His recovery had better be quick. He wasn't sure how much time alone with her he could handle. She was within his reach and so tempting. Now that he had had a taste of her, he wanted more. Much more.

***

The sun was well up when Strykes woke and staggered from the bedroom. Now that he could get up and about, she had insisted that he take her room, and she slept in the chair. He knew it wasn't comfortable for her, but no matter how much he wanted it, it wasn't proper for them to share the bed.

"Good afternoon," she greeted from the kitchen.

She stood at the counter with a dozen jars before her. She appeared to be placing dried leaves into them. Herb jars, he supposed.

"Afternoon." He headed for the coffeepot left warming on the stove. He eagerly poured himself a cup.

"Thought you were going to sleep all day."

"I could. Your bed is comfortable."

"How is your shoulder?"

"Hurts." He took a drink of coffee and made a face at the bitterness. "What happened to the coffee?"

She smiled and held up one of the jars. "I put this in it. It will help with the pain."

"Wonderful," he muttered as he took another drink.

Outside, Saber barked, and Strykes went to the window and looked out. A man on a buckskin horse was riding toward the cabin.

"It's Hank." He turned to look at her. "Why is he coming here?" he asked as a surge of jealousy went through him.

She scowled at his tone. "Probably to get something for the pain in his leg from where you shot him."

"*I* wasn't the one that shot him."

"You didn't stop it from happening either. Go hide in the bedroom."

Strykes grumbled and took his coffee with him as he went into the small room. She grabbed the curtain and pulled it closed. He was sure that if it had been a door, she would have slammed it.

LaRisa glared at the curtain and then turned to the door. She did her best to compose herself and look as if she wasn't hiding a man in her bedroom.

When there was a knock on her door, she calmly walked to it and opened it to reveal Hank standing there. He wore his buckskins and knee-high moccasins. His brown eyes were friendly as he nodded a greeting.

"Hello, Hank."

"Miss Reeves, I came for more of the herbs you gave me," he told her. "They've been working good on my leg."

"Glad to hear it."

LaRisa went to her little herb cupboard in the kitchen. She removed a small square of cloth and string. Going to the counter and her jars, she picked one up and poured an amount onto the cloth. She drew the edges up and tied the string around it to make a little pouch.

She turned to Hank, who still stood in the doorway. "This should last about a month."

"Thank you." Hank took the pouch from her. He stilled, and his eyes went to the closed bedroom curtain. "Who else is here?" he asked suspiciously, his hand going to the big knife on his belt.

"It's nobody, Hank," LaRisa lied.

"I heard someone in there."

"No, there isn't anyone—"

"It's all right, LaRisa," Strykes said as he pushed back the curtain and came into the room, coffee cup in hand.

Hank's dark eyes went flat, and his body tensed. "What the hell are you doing here?"

"He's hiding," LaRisa blurted. "Strykes was attacked and nearly killed. He came here, and I helped him."

Hank studied Strykes for a moment. His body relaxed, but his hand stayed near his knife. "You're the reason those men are out there watching every trail in and out of town."

LaRisa felt her heart stutter. "How many are there?"

"I don't know, but someone followed me all the way here, and I saw someone watching the road when I rode into town yesterday." He fixed Strykes with a hard look. "Is Miss Reeves in danger?"

"As long as they don't find out I'm here." Strykes appeared to think something over before he spoke. "It's some of the same men that tried to kill you last year."

Something close to hatred filled Hank's eyes. "They've come back?"

Strykes nodded and gestured to the table, inviting the man to sit and talk for a while. "To kill me."

LaRisa went to the stove and poured Hank a cup of coffee before she joined them at the table. "They nearly did kill you," she informed Strykes.

"A while back, when you were attacked and nearly died, Boone and I killed the gang leader and several of their men. But Lucas, the gang's second-in-command, escaped and swore vengeance on me for killing Brown. He's finally come to make good his threat. The coward ambushed me and nearly had me dead."

Hank nodded before he took a long drink of coffee. "Now they're out there looking for you to finish the job."

"He won't be happy until he's standing over my dead body."

"Boone know 'bout this?" Hank asked.

"He does."

"I'll talk to Boone and do what I can to help. I want that bastard Lucas dead. He's the one that shot me."

Strykes nodded. "I'm sure Boone would appreciate the help."

Hank finished his coffee and looked at LaRisa. "Thank you for the herbs."

LaRisa stood and walked him to the door. "Be careful on your ride to town."

"I will," he said simply, and he left the cabin.

LaRisa closed the door behind him and returned to the table to sit with Strykes. "It's good to know that there is another man out there helping to keep you safe."

Strykes let out a long breath and leaned back in his chair. "At the risk of his own life. Hank nearly died because of Brown's gang. I may have killed Brown, but Lucas wants revenge, and I'd hate to see Hank get hurt again."

LaRisa nodded in understanding. "But this time he won't be taken by surprise. They ambushed him last time."

He gave her a humorless grin. "Lucas is good at ambushes. He doesn't have the guts to face a fair fight. If he finds out I'm here, he'll ambush this place, and we'll both be dead."

LaRisa tried not to let her fear show. She knew he was right.

Chapter Nine

LaRisa busied herself with preparing the evening meal and tried to ignore Strykes as he paced restlessly. She had found herself looking at him far too often and thinking things she shouldn't. The attraction she felt for him was growing, and it was something she had to get under control.

"Do you need any help?" Strykes asked as he walked to her.

She turned from the counter and looked at him with curious eyes. "You know how to cook?"

"Well, you don't have to sound so shocked."

She let out a small laugh. "I didn't mean to. You just don't seem the type to know your way around a kitchen."

"My mother worked as a cook for ten years, so I picked up a few things here and there."

LaRisa bit her lip a moment against the many questions she wanted to ask him. She knew almost nothing about him. All she knew was that he came from the South and was part of a gang of outlaws for a long time. Thankfully, there was no proof of Strykes doing any of the illegal activity that the gang had been involved in, and Travis hadn't arrested him. He appeared to have accepted his current life and had put his past behind him until Lucas had returned.

"I can hear you thinking," he told her with humor.

His voice startled LaRisa, but she somehow kept herself composed. "I-I was just wondering where you were from. Boone said he knew you in Missouri. Is that where you were born?"

Strykes pulled in a deep breath and said nothing for a moment. "Louisiana. My folks worked on a plantation there. Ma cooked for the family that owned the plantation. Pa was the overseer, and he was a cruel man."

LaRisa heard the regret in his voice and wasn't sure she wanted to pry any further. It was clear that there were many unpleasant memories going through his head. She had heard stories of how the slaves were treated before the war had freed them. Rimrock had been affected very little during the war, though several of her cousins had enlisted to fight for the North.

"Were you in the war?" she asked hesitantly.

He looked at her for a moment. "Yeah."

"For the South?"

"Yeah. Is that a problem?" His voice was carefully controlled, but tension radiated from him.

She shook her head. "No. The war was a bad thing no matter what side you were on. Men fought for what they believed."

"I fought to survive," he told her flatly before he focused on cooking once again. "Just having a southern accent made a man a target for every Yank out there. My friend and I joined up with the militia and dove right into hell."

"Strykes, I-I'm sorry. I shouldn't have asked," she said regretfully.

"It's fine," he told her gently. "We're stuck in here together." He gestured at the tiny space of the cabin. "It's normal to talk about things. So, it's my turn to ask questions."

LaRisa felt her heart jump. She didn't want him to ask her anything. "Strykes, I don't—"

"Have you ever been courted?" he asked flatly as he looked at her.

Her eyes went wide, and for a moment she had trouble breathing. "N-no."

"Why?"

She swallowed hard. "Nobody ever...I'm not...I don't want to talk about this."

LaRisa turned from him and headed for the door. She needed air and time to calm herself. She had never expected Strykes to ask such a question, and it frustrated her that she couldn't give him an answer. Of course she had never been courted. Every man in town was afraid of her and kept their distance. Every man except Strykes.

She reached the door at the same time he reached her. A big hand clamped down on her arm to keep her from opening the door. He turned her to face him and took her shoulders to hold her pressed to the door, effectively keeping her from escaping.

"LaRisa, I'm sorry," he told her softly. "It's none of my business. I didn't mean to make you uncomfortable."

"I don't want to talk about it." She could hear the desperation in her voice as the familiar longing settled in.

"I just find it hard to believe that a woman as beautiful as you are doesn't have—"

"I'm not beautiful," she corrected him.

His hand lifted to cup her cheek and make her look at him. "The hell you're not."

LaRisa swallowed hard as she looked up into his eyes. Did he really think she was beautiful?

His mouth slowly lowered to hers, and the kiss was gentle. A small shudder of pleasure went through her as she kissed him back.

A low sound rumbled in his chest as he slid his arms around her to pull her close and deepened the kiss. Her arms went around his neck, and her hands fisted tightly in his shirt. The need to touch him was great, but she couldn't risk it. The feelings he was creating inside her were unfamiliar, and fear threatened. She could hurt him. Or worse.

Outside, Saber barked, and Strykes muttered a curse as he lifted his head and went to the window. LaRisa stood there leaning against the door, trying to compose herself and get her heart to calm.

"It's your ma," he told her as he stood to the side and peered through the edge of the curtain.

"My ma!"

LaRisa ran her hands over her hair and straightened her bodice. She wasn't sure what good any of it would do because the guilt that would no doubt be on her face would give away the fact that she had just been kissing a man she had no business kissing.

She ignored the chuckle from Strykes as she whirled around and opened the door. She walked into the yard and waited for her mother. The buggy drew closer as the brown horse trotted along easily, and Saber loped down the road to greet the visitor.

LaRisa hoped she looked composed as her mother pulled the horse to a halt. "Good evening, Mama."

Shyfawn smiled as she stepped down from the carriage. "You seem pleasantly chipper today."

"So far it's been a good day," LaRisa said with a smile.

Shyfawn returned her smile as she quickly tied the horse to the little tree in the yard. "I brought you and your guest a few things."

Shyfawn reached into the buggy and pulled out a basket covered with a checked cloth. LaRisa led the way into the cabin. She waited for her mother to enter before closing the door.

"Good afternoon, Mr. Strykes," Shyfawn greeted. "You're looking well."

He nodded. "I'm feeling well too. I'm ready to get out of here, but LaRisa doesn't think it's safe yet."

"And she's right," Shyfawn said matter-of-factly. "On my way here, I saw a rider in the trees. He followed me all the way here. They're watching this place."

Strykes muttered a curse as he rammed his fingers through his hair. "That's not good. No telling how long they'll be watching either."

"Don't fret too much," Shyfawn told him. "Travis got back a few days ago, and he and Heck are watching them."

Strykes nodded. "That does make me feel a little better." That much was true. If they were out there watching for him, he wanted backup out there to help keep LaRisa safe.

"Here." Shyfawn dug into the basket and tossed him a small bundle. "Roper thought you'd be needing this."

Strykes caught the bundle and opened it. He grinned and pulled out the makings for a smoke. "I'll work for free for a month for this."

LaRisa shot him a glare. "Not in my cabin," she informed him.

He gave her a smirk and stuffed it in his pocket. "We'll see."

"I also brought a pie and bread." She removed the cloth from the basket to reveal the goodies she had brought.

LaRisa gathered plates and forks. Then the three sat at the table and each enjoyed a slice of pie.

Shyfawn stayed for quite a while, and LaRisa enjoyed the visit. She didn't see her parents enough and didn't realize just how much she missed them.

"I should get going before it gets dark," Shyfawn said as she stood, picking up the now-empty basket.

Strykes stood and patted a hand on his stomach. "Thank you, Mrs. Reeves. It was delicious."

She smiled at him. "I'm glad you liked it. I'll tell Sam that you are much improved."

LaRisa walked out to the buggy with her mother. "I'm glad you came by."

"Me too. I miss you."

Unexpected tears burned her eyes. "I miss you too. Be careful going home."

"Travis and Heck will have an eye on the men, so don't worry."

LaRisa let out a breath. "That makes me feel better knowing they are looking out for us."

"If there is any kind of trouble, you get to the caves. Nobody will be able to follow you through them."

She nodded. "I'll use them if I have to."

Shyfawn placed the basket on the buggy seat. "Strykes." Her tone was serious. "Are you all right being alone here with him?"

Shyfawn felt her face flush at the meaning behind her mother's words. "Yes." She nodded. "He's been a gentleman." Mostly, she silently added.

"If he tries to hurt you, shoot him," Shyfawn said flatly.

LaRisa gave a snort. "If that man decides to hurt me, I won't have a chance to get to a gun. He's a lot bigger than I am, and he's not stupid. Besides, I don't need a gun to kill him," she said sadly.

"LaRisa, honey…" Shyfawn reached up to embrace her daughter, but LaRisa took a step back. Hurt showed on Shyfawn's face, and she folded her hands before her. "Don't think like that."

She took a deep breath. "I'm sorry, Mama."

Shyfawn nodded and climbed into the buggy. She gathered up the reins and smiled at LaRisa. "I'll see you again soon."

"Thank you for coming," she told her, and she meant it. She rarely received visitors, and her parents respected her need to be alone and didn't visit too often.

"I love you, sweetheart."

"Love you too, Mama," she said and felt her throat grow tight.

Shyfawn slapped the reins on the horse, and the buggy rattled away. LaRisa stood there and watched her mother fade into the distance. Saber trotted after the buggy for a short distance, then sat down on the trail to watch it continue down the road. LaRisa loved her parents so much. They had been so understanding with her decision to live secluded and never tried to push her into a life she wasn't comfortable with. She sighed and walked back to her cabin.

LaRisa entered the cabin to the powerful smell of cigarette smoke. "Strykes!" she snapped as she saw him seated at the table, taking a long drag.

"Yes?" his voice held a hint of humor as he gave her a smirk. In his exhale, he blew a smoke ring at her.

LaRisa clenched her fists at her sides. "Put that out," she demanded. "Or I'll do it for you."

LaRisa fought back anger when Strykes gave her a look that said "I dare you" as he took another drag. She let out a muttered curse and shot him a hard look as she marched past him. Those men out there better leave or catch him, because she was about to kill him herself.

Chapter Ten

Strykes savored the taste of the smoke as it burned into his lungs. He knew LaRisa was furious with him, but it was worth facing her wrath. He would love Shyfawn forever for bringing him the package. His body relaxed as he let the smoke leave his lungs slowly.

He bellowed when water suddenly came at him, effectively putting out the cigarette and soaking the tobacco pouch in his shirt pocket.

"What the hell?" he growled as he jumped to his feet.

LaRisa stood there, her face angry and an empty pan in her hands. "I said put that out."

Strykes clenched his teeth as he dropped the useless cigarette onto the tabletop and wiped the water from his face with a jerk. "That was a mean thing to do." He pulled the wet tobacco pouch from his shirt pocket and plopped it on the table. "We could go to war over this."

"Then you better grab up an army," she informed him as she held the pan up.

"I won't be needing an army." He took a step toward her.

"You stay away from me," she said, holding the pan out in front of her like a shield. His pale eyes snapped with anger, and she took a step back. "Strykes, I'm warning you." She tried to sound brave.

He almost laughed. "Really?"

She shrieked as he made a dive for her, and she tried to run. A powerful arm wrapped around her waist, nearly lifting her from the floor as his free hand snatched the pan from her grasp. It clattered to the floor as he hauled her toward the water pitcher.

"Don't you dare!" she hollered at him, doing her best to wiggle out of his grasp.

Strykes's hand went around the water pitcher as he threw her to the floor. She gave a yelp and tried to scramble away from him. He grabbed her and rolled her onto her back, straddling her as he sat down on her thighs. He grabbed both her wrists in one hand and held them tightly to his chest as he hung the pitcher over her face.

"Strykes, get off me before I hurt you," she snapped.

He couldn't hold back his laughter. "Don't think I need that army after all." He tipped the pitcher up and let a bit of water dribble out onto her forehead.

"Strykes!" she hollered and did her best to get out of his hold as the water dripped down on her. "I'm going to kill you."

He laughed. "Gather your army." He then tipped the pitcher and poured water over her head.

LaRisa squeezed her eyes shut and held her breath as the water came down over her. "You bastard!" she sputtered.

Strykes set the pitcher aside and pushed the wet strands of hair from her face. "Give up yet?" he asked her, his voice full of humor.

She glared up at him. "You're going to be sorry for this."

He smiled and released her wrists. Resting a hand on either side of her head, he leaned over her. "Somehow I doubt it." Unable to stop himself, he leaned down and brushed his lips over hers. "I'd say it was worth it," he said before he claimed her mouth fully.

LaRisa stiffened and held her breath as his mouth slid over hers. What the hell? A second ago, he was trying to drown her, and now he was kissing her. Her anger faded as his mouth teased over hers. She let her breath out in a sigh and opened her mouth to him.

Strykes groaned and kissed her deeply. When he had started the water fight, he had only meant to get even with her for putting out his cigarette. He sure as hell hadn't planned on this. He didn't know why he had kissed her. As long as she wasn't arguing, he would just keep on doing it. She tasted so good, and her mouth was so hot and inviting.

Her hands went to his chest to push him away, but they fisted into the material of his wet shirt. She held on tightly, trying to pull him even closer as he devoured her lips. She shifted beneath him, and a sound rumbled in his chest. His mouth never left hers as he lifted off her to lie beside her, resting on one elbow as he leaned over her. His hand went to her waist and pulled her against him. Pain shot through his shoulder, but he ignored it. He would not let a little pain keep him from kissing this perfect woman.

LaRisa made a soft noise as her fingers wound in his hair, pulling his mouth harder against hers. Her body was on fire everywhere it touched his. His mouth on hers created a hot churning in her stomach that spread out over her body. Never in all her life had she ever imagined kissing a man could be like this. It was all so overwhelming; it terrified her, yet she wanted more.

When he could no longer breathe, Strykes pulled back and looked at her. Both were breathing hard, and he felt her body trembling. He almost laughed when he realized he, too, was a bit shaky. Her emerald eyes were glazed with a passion that made her look so damn inviting. Her cheeks were flushed, and her lips were swollen from his kisses. He lightly stroked her cheek with the backs of his fingers.

"I hope you've learned your lesson," he said a bit breathlessly. "You gonna try another sneak attack again?"

She smiled at him. "If I told you, it wouldn't be very sneaky."

He gave her a soft kiss. "That's true."

Strykes moved off her and sat back on his heels. He let out a long breath as he tried to get his body under control. She was so damn tempting lying there on the floor. He got to his feet and held out a hand to her. She reluctantly took it, and he helped her to her feet.

She busied her shaking hands smoothing down her dress. Her heart still thundered in her chest; she was sure he could hear it. She wiped the water from her face and smoothed back the wet strands of hair.

When she looked at Strykes, her breath caught. He pulled his wet shirt off and hung it over the kitchen chair to dry. LaRisa watched as he moved, his muscles rippling. She had seen him without his shirt before. She had undressed him. This was entirely different.

Strykes turned to see her staring at him with wide eyes. "You all right?" he asked as he stepped toward her.

"Fine," she said a little too quickly. Her voice sounded breathless.

He gave her a small grin. "You should probably get out of your wet things too." He took another step toward her. "I can help if you need me to."

She felt her cheeks redden. "Absolutely not."

He stepped up to her until he was only inches away. "After all, you did undress me." He reached out and fingered a button on her bodice. "I could return the favor."

She swallowed hard and tried not to think of his bare chest as it almost begged to be touched. "You were shot and bloody. I had to undress you."

He grunted and thought for a moment. "So you're saying…" He leaned over and nuzzled her neck, kissing and sipping the water droplets from her skin. "I'm going to have to shoot you to get you out of your clothes."

Much to her own shock, LaRisa burst into laughter. "Yes, but don't you dare try it." Unable to stop herself, she wound her arms around his neck and hugged him to her.

Strykes pulled her close and chuckled against her neck. "Talk about a blow to a man's ego." He pulled back and looked into her dancing eyes. "I'll just have to think of another way, I guess."

She gave him a wide smile. "I would appreciate that."

He gave her a quick kiss and stepped away from her. If he didn't put some distance between them, he was going to throw her down and take her right there. Her smile and laughter only made him want her more. He went to get some rags and cleaned up the mess of water all around the kitchen. He had to keep his hands busy and keep his eyes on something besides her for a little while.

LaRisa couldn't keep her eyes from following him around the cabin. Her gaze riveted on his back and chest. She wanted to run her hands over the dusting of hair across his chest. Her eyes followed the hair to where it disappeared into his pants. Her face flushed as she remembered undressing and bathing him. She took a deep breath and turned away from him. Her mind was having thoughts that scared the hell out of her.

"Your bandages are soaked," she said and turned to him again. "I'll have to change them."

With unsteady hands, LaRisa changed the bandages on his shoulder. This day had been one surprise after another. The passionate kisses they had shared filled her mind as she worked. She had never imagined that kissing a man would be so wonderful.

"What are you smiling about?" he asked, though there was a knowing in his voice.

An embarrassed flush crept over her cheeks. "I didn't realize I was."

She quickly finished and turned away from him, placing the soiled bandages on the floor near the stove. She would wash them later, but for now, she would get dinner ready. She wasn't hungry, having had the pie not long ago, but she needed to stay busy.

All too soon, the day was over, and they were getting ready for bed. She stood in her bedroom, changing into her nightdress. Another night spent with Strykes.

LaRisa emerged from her bedroom in her nightdress, a blanket wrapped around her. A silly effort to keep Strykes from seeing her nightdress.

"Are you sure you want to sleep out here?" he asked.

"Where else would I sleep?"

Strykes grinned at her.

"No. Don't even think like that," she informed him as she felt her face heat.

"Fine. Dash my hopes. Good night."

"Good night."

She watched him disappear into the bedroom and pull the curtain. A sigh left her as she went about making a place to sleep on the table. The chair was terribly uncomfortable to sleep on, and she had no desire to sleep on the floor.

When her blankets and pillows were to her liking, she crawled up on the table and did her best to get comfortable. Impossible. Sleeping in her bed would be preferable, but Strykes needed to sleep there. The soft bed and good sleep would help him be comfortable and heal.

Had he really suggested that she sleep with him? A strange feeling went through her body at the thought of sharing a bed with him. What would it be like? Would he kiss her again?

She grumbled under her breath and curled up in her blankets. Sleep would be elusive if she couldn't stop thinking about him, though she knew when sleep finally took her, he would be in her dreams.

In the bedroom, Strykes lay staring up at the ceiling. The moonlight cast shadows over the room as he shifted restlessly on the bed. It would be big enough for the both of them. Did he dare?

With a curse, Strykes got out of bed and padded on bare feet to the curtain. Quietly, he pushed it back to see LaRisa sleeping on the top of the table. That couldn't be comfortable. She would sleep much better in her bed. And he would sleep better with her in his arms. He walked toward the table.

"LaRisa."

She yelped at the sound of his harsh voice. She turned to him as his arms slid under her. He lifted her and cradled her against his chest before he turned and walked to the bedroom.

"Strykes." She pushed at him. "Your shoulder."

"It's fine," he lied.

"Strykes, what are you doing?" she demanded.

"Be quiet," he snapped and laid her on the bed. He arranged the blankets over her and slid in beside her.

"Strykes!" She tried to scoot away from him, but his arms were around her in an instant. "We can't sleep together."

"Why not?" he asked. "It's your cabin, so there is no reason for you to be uncomfortable on the table," he informed her as he drew her close.

"Maybe so, but you don't need to sleep with me."

A chuckle rumbled in his chest. "Sure I do. I'm hurt, and I need to be comfortable as well." His arms tightened around her. "I think this will do. Now"—he put a hand on her head and pressed it against his shoulder—"go to sleep."

"Strykes, this isn't proper," she grumbled at him.

He chuckled. "I won't tell if you won't."

She growled in frustration. "Damn it, get out of—"

"LaRisa," he interrupted. "I've been here alone with you for a while now. Any gossip that is going on has started. I'm glad for your concern, but you've already damaged my reputation."

"Your reputation?" She couldn't stop the laughter that escaped her. "You're impossible."

"I know." He settled back and held her close. "Let's just sleep tonight in comfort, and tomorrow you can cuss me some more."

LaRisa smiled and settled against him. "You bet your ass I will."

He gasped. "Such language. We'll have to work on your pillow talk."

She laughed. "Just when did you develop this sense of humor?"

He thought for a moment. She was right. He hadn't joked or even laughed in so long he had almost forgotten what it was like. Since his arrival here and staying with her, he had changed. Being here with her, he was at ease and relaxed. Jesus, he was happy. For the first time since he was seventeen, he was truly happy.

"Go to sleep," he said roughly.

She gave a snort. "Guess I spoke too soon. And nobody knows you're here, so nobody is gossiping about us."

"Minor detail. Now sleep."

He had to bite back a groan as she shifted against him to get more comfortable. Soon her breathing was slow and even as she slept. He stayed awake long into the night, just enjoying the act of holding her close.

Chapter Eleven

The sun was well up when Strykes was drawn from his sleep by the smell of coffee and cooking. He quickly pulled on his trousers and left the bedroom. He was eager to see LaRisa.

Strykes stood in the bedroom doorway, drinking in the sight of her. Jesus, she was beautiful. How in the hell had this happened to him? She turned and smiled at him. He was more than halfway in love with her, and that was a dangerous thing.

"It's about time you woke up." Her smile faded, and she crossed the room to him. "Your shoulder," she said as she examined the bloody bandage. "Sit down and let me tend to it."

He did as she ordered. He sat on the table and watched her as she quickly grabbed water and fresh bandages. She returned and immediately went to work. Her face was serious, and her green eyes focused as she carefully removed the bloody bandage.

"It's your fault," he said quietly.

She snorted. "I didn't ask you to pick me up."

"Not that."

She met his eyes. "Then what is my fault?"

"The sense of humor I have suddenly developed." He reached up and pulled at a strand of her auburn hair.

"How can that be my fault?" She focused on cleaning his shoulder wound. He had torn it open when he had carried her to the bed.

"Because I was a perfectly miserable bastard until you came along." He rested his hands on her waist, and she looked at him. "I don't know what you've done to me, but it's confusing as hell."

She gave him a soft smile. "Yes, it is."

***

Strykes paced the cabin restlessly. He felt if he spent one more day in the small confines of the cabin, he would go crazy. He enjoyed his time spent with LaRisa. Getting to know her wasn't easy, but he liked her all the same. She kept a lot of things guarded inside. Of course, so did he.

Strykes watched as she brushed her hair, her arm making long fluid motions. Without a word, he stood and went over to her. She gave a start when he put his hand on hers. He took the brush from her and began running it through her hair. With every brush, he ran his fingers the length of it, letting the silky smoothness slide through his fingers.

LaRisa sat stock still as he brushed her hair. She was unsure of what to do. She should probably stop him, yet just how would she do that? He was a mountain of a man. It wasn't like she could just shove him away. Soon her body relaxed, and her eyes closed as she enjoyed the feel of his hands in her hair.

She wasn't aware of how much time had passed when he set aside the brush and braided her hair. He held out his hand, and she placed the ribbon in his palm. He tied the ribbon in place, then ran the length of the braid through his hands before letting it fall down her back.

"Thank you," LaRisa said in an unsteady voice.

"It's been a long time since I've done that," Strykes said softly.

"Really?" She felt an unexpected pang of jealousy. She stood and went to the kitchen, organizing the already-organized cooking pots. "You often run around braiding women's hair?"

Strykes suppressed a smile. "Well, not exactly. However, I enjoyed braiding yours much more."

She snorted and folded her arms. "I guess that's all that matters, right?" When she turned, he was standing close to her.

He reached out and pulled her braid over her shoulder. "Yes." His eyes held hers. "I've never brushed or braided a woman's hair before."

She frowned at him. "But you just said—"

"My sisters," he interrupted. "When they were girls."

LaRisa felt herself flush red and lowered her eyes. She felt foolish for being jealous. What was wrong with her? She barely knew him, and it shouldn't matter to her what he had done or who he had done it with.

He let the braid slip through his fingers, and his hand went to her face, making her look at him. His thumb lightly trailed across her bottom lip, and his hand moved along her jaw to cup the back of her head. She watched as he lowered his head, her eyes focused on his mouth. He tilted her face to his and lightly kissed her lips.

LaRisa's air left her lungs, and she leaned into him, placing her hands on his chest. He pulled back for a moment and looked at her, his pale eyes searching her emerald. He muttered a curse and captured her lips fully. His arms went around her, and he pulled her against him. She wound her arms around his neck and opened her mouth to him. He groaned and tightened his hold on her, deepening the kiss.

Strykes couldn't stop the shudder that went through his body when she made a soft noise and pressed herself against him. She felt so good in his arms, her mouth on his, her fingers wound tightly in his hair. His arms tightened around her, and he lifted her from the floor, carrying her the few steps to the table. He sat her down on the tabletop and pushed her legs apart with his thighs to stand between them.

She gave a small gasp when his hands went to her hips, and he pulled her tightly against him. His hands then slid up her body to work at the buttons of her bodice. He had to touch her soft skin. It was a need he couldn't explain, but he couldn't get his shaking fingers to work fast enough. He gripped the front of her bodice with both hands and ripped it open, sending buttons flying.

She gave a startled cry, but he swallowed it in his kiss as he shoved her bodice open to caress her breasts. Jesus, she wasn't wearing anything beneath her bodice. She moaned against his mouth as his thumbs trailed over her peaked nipples.

Strykes couldn't stop the low growl that rumbled in his chest. Her breasts where even fuller than he had imagined, and Lord knew he thought about them a lot. They fit his large hands perfectly, firm and yet so damn soft. She deepened the kiss and pushed herself against his hands as he explored her. Her skin was like silk under his rough hands, and heat rushed through his body in a violent wave.

His mouth never left hers as he laid her back across the table and covered her with his body. Damn, it felt so right to have her beneath him. His mouth left hers to close over her sweet nipple to suckle and tug. She cried out, and her fingers went to his hair to hold him to her. His mouth and hands moved over her breasts and her moan of pleasure was music to his ears. But he wanted more.

He gave her nipple a gentle bite before he lifted and kissed her deeply as a hand went to her leg. Lifting it, he worked the hem of her dress up until he touched her bare thigh. His other hand worked the layers of her dress to bunch at her waist. Both his hands slid up her bare thighs to caress her hips. God, she was so soft. His large hands held her hips tight as he pushed his arousal against her.

"Strykes?" she breathed against his lips.

At the sound of her shaky voice, he pulled back and looked down into her eyes. They were glazed with passion but also held a touch of fear. Her lips were swollen from his kisses, her cheeks flushed.

What the hell was he doing? He had let his passion cloud his good sense. He was all set to take her right here across the table. Jesus, she deserved better than that. His eyes moved to her torn bodice, and he felt his gut twist until he thought he would be sick.

"God, LaRisa." His voice was ragged. "I'm sorry."

Strykes let go of her hips and pulled her dress back down. He helped her sit up. He found a button on her bodice had survived, and he fastened it to cover her breasts. He stepped back and pushed her thighs closed as he fought down sudden panic. She wasn't safe with him. But he had known that all along.

He couldn't look at her as he rammed his fingers through his hair and tried to turn away from her. It was then he realized she had a tight grip on the front of his shirt. He took a deep breath and placed his shaking hands over hers and held them tight. He squeezed his eyes shut and did his best to calm the raging passion and shame he felt.

"Strykes?" she said again, her voice steadier.

He let the breath he had been holding out slowly and met her eyes. They were shimmering with unshed tears as she gave him a questioning look. He muttered a curse and pulled her into his arms and held her shaking body tightly.

"I'm so sorry," he whispered against her hair. "I was completely out of line." He pulled back and held her face in his hands. "But you have no idea what you do to me. You don't know how bad this need I have for you is," he said regretfully as he placed a light kiss on her lips. "I don't want to hurt you."

She swallowed hard. "You weren't hurting me." She couldn't stop the tears that escaped down her cheeks.

Strykes felt a sudden tightness in his chest. Unable to speak, he kissed her tears away before he captured her lips. He kissed her gently, and she kissed him back without hesitation. Her arms went around his waist and held on tightly. He broke the kiss and held her against his chest. He let out a shuddering breath and kissed the top of her head.

"Don't be sorry," she whispered as she listened to his strong heartbeat. "I'm not."

Strykes had to stifle an agonized groan. "If we hadn't stopped, you might feel differently. You deserve someone better than me."

"Somehow I doubt that," she said and nestled closer to his chest.

"Believe me, I'm not the kind of man you want to get mixed up with."

She looked up at him. "I think we're mixed up whether you like it or not."

He gave her a small smile. "Never said I didn't like it."

She nuzzled against his chest again. "If we spend too much more time together here, we won't be able to fight it anymore."

He pulled her close. She was right, and he knew it. Every day that passed, it was getting harder to keep his hands off her. Each time he touched her and kissed her made it more intense, and the need was getting the better of his good judgment. She didn't realize just what would happen between them, and she might end up regretting it and hating him. She could hate him for so many reasons, and he could possibly hurt her in so many ways. God, if he ever hurt her, he would never forgive himself.

"Now is not the time to try and figure out what's happening between us." He kissed her on the head again. "I've got people trying to kill me. I think we should wait until everything is safe before we try to figure out our feelings."

"When will it be safe?" She couldn't stop the catch in her voice.

"I don't know," he said honestly.

It might never be safe for him. He had done a lot in his past, and a lot of people might come looking to kill him. He had a past that could kill her. Hell, *he* could kill her.

Chapter Twelve

LaRisa watched Strykes as he sat in the chair, his eyes focused on the darkness outside the window. It had been two days since he had kissed her, and he had been distant. His conversations with her comprised short answers and grunts, though at night, he would hold her so tightly and not let her go until morning.

She cocked her head to the side and looked at him. "Aren't you coming to bed?"

He stretched his legs out in front of him. "Nope."

She frowned. "Why?"

"I don't think it would be a good idea," he told her as he settled back in the chair.

"Now?" she fairly snapped. "You've decided it's a bad idea *now*?"

He shot her a hard look. "Yes."

"It's a little late for that." She couldn't stop the feeling of hurt that went through her. "You've been fine with it for the last several nights."

"I've changed my mind," he told her as he rested his head back. "Go to bed."

"Strykes, you can't just come into my house, turn my life upside down, sleep in my bed with me, and change your mind suddenly." She glared at him as he relaxed into the chair. "What the hell is wrong with you?"

In an instant, Strykes was on his feet and jerked her body against his. She cried out and pushed at his chest. He held her tightly with one arm around her, and a hand fisted in her hair, forcing her head back to look at him. Her eyes were wide with alarm as his hard eyes drilled into hers.

"*You* are what's wrong with me." He practically growled the words out. "I want you, LaRisa. Sleeping next to you at night is killing me. One of these nights you are going to wake up, and I will be on top of you."

Her heart pounded as she realized what he meant. He wanted to take her body. It was a fight for him to control that feeling, and he was losing that fight.

He lowered his mouth and lightly brushed her lips. "I want you under me, and I want to be buried inside you as deep as I can get." His voice was rough as his mouth went to her neck.

LaRisa gasped at the rush of heat that went through her. She could only look at him when his hard eyes met hers again. The hunger in their clear depths made her stomach clench. He pulled her closer, and she felt the hardness of his arousal against her hip.

He tightened his hold on her hair and tipped her head farther back. "I want you screaming and begging for more."

LaRisa could only stare at him in shock. She opened her mouth to speak, but nothing came out.

With a muttered curse, he let her go and stepped back.

"Go to bed, LaRisa," he ordered and sank back down in the chair.

She couldn't move for a long time as she thought of his words. Somehow, she got her body to obey her, and she turned from him to go to her bed and crawl in. She pulled the blankets up to her chin as she curled up tight on her side, facing away from Strykes. Her bed felt big and lonely as she struggled to fall asleep.

She rolled over and tried to see him. He had put out the lamps, and she had a difficult time finding him in the dim moonlight coming in through the windows. She could barely make out his outline as he rested in the chair. She wanted him in bed with her, and she wanted his arms around her.

LaRisa didn't understand how it was possible for someone she barely knew and had only spent a few weeks with could have affected her so greatly. That wasn't entirely true. Strykes had affected her the first time she had seen him. Something inside her told her she needed him in her life.

LaRisa tossed again and let out a frustrated sigh before she stood and padded on bare feet to where Strykes lounged in the chair. Her eyes moved over him, and she stepped closer. Everything about him called to her, and for the first time in her adult life, she needed someone. She had prepared herself to be alone for the rest of her life, and Strykes had changed everything for her.

LaRisa swallowed hard and found her voice. "Strykes, I—"

"Go back to bed," he told her, not opening his eyes. If he opened them and saw her, he would be lost. "You should be asleep."

"I want you to sleep with me," she told him softly.

Strykes dared to look at her as he shifted in the chair to sit up. As he knew, she was beautiful standing there in the moonlight wearing her nightdress. "We talked about this."

She said nothing as she moved to him to sit across his lap and rested her head on his chest. He had to grip the arms of the chair tightly to keep from wrapping his arms around her and holding her close. He had been sitting in this damn chair for hours wishing he was in bed holding her, and it had taken everything he had not to go to her.

"What're you doing?" he growled.

She was silent for a long time. Finally, she raised her head and ran her hand along his whiskered jaw. "I want to completely ruin your reputation."

The air slammed out of his lungs, and he stared at her. "What?"

"I-I want to be under you," she said, feeling her cheeks flush. "I want you deep inside me."

Strykes felt a fist twist in his gut as his heart pounded. He took her face in his hands. "Are you sure?"

She nodded. "Yes, I'm sure."

"It won't be slow and gentle like you deserve. I need you too badly to take my time. It's going to be rough and fast, and when we get started, I won't be able to stop," he told her regretfully as his eyes searched hers in the dim light of the moon. "You have to be *very* sure you want this."

She swallowed hard, and heat flooded her body at the sound of the urgent need in his voice. "I'm very sure."

Strykes swore and pulled her mouth to his. He kissed her with all the passion he possessed. She eagerly opened her mouth to him, and he took advantage of it. He shifted her until she was straddling him.

In one swift motion, he pulled her nightdress off over her head and flung it aside. His hands and mouth instantly went to her breasts, and she cried out when he took a nipple into his mouth.

LaRisa arched against him as his mouth tugged at her. Heat shot through her body, and she wound her fingers in his hair, holding him to her. A low sound came from him, and her stomach clenched. She tugged at his shirt, the need to feel him overwhelming her. He drew back and pulled his shirt off and flung it away. She ran her hands over his chest and pressed against him as she took his mouth.

He muttered some kind of curse, and she let out a gasp when their naked skin met. His hands moved over her back, holding her close as he kissed her deeply. Jesus, she was so damn soft.

He ran his hands over her skin and savored the feel of her. She gave a startled gasp when he wrapped his arms around her and stood.

"Wrap your legs around me," he ordered.

She did as he said, and he carried her to the bed. He laid her down and covered her body with his as he kissed her deeply. A low groan came from him when she kept her legs locked around him, and his body ached painfully for hers. Every fantasy he had ever had about her went through his mind, and he intended to start with exploring every inch of her body.

She breathed a protest when he drew back, and she was forced to release her legs. "Where are you going?" she asked, her voice breathless.

Strykes said nothing as he left the bed and reached for the lamp and lit it. Placing it on the shelf, he turned and looked at her as she sat up in bed and crossed her arms over her breasts. He knew she would be a bit shy, but she was going to have to get over that in a hurry. She watched him with wide eyes as he moved to the bed. He stopped.

"What is it?" she asked with worry.

He gave her a slight grin. "I think I better put Saber outside. I'd hate for him to bite me on the ass for what I'm about to do to you."

Strykes called the dog, and the animal followed him to the door. He let the dog out and stepped outside to breathe in the crisp night air. It helped calm him a little. He was about to make love to LaRisa.

Closing the door, he returned to the bed. She watched him as he pulled off his pants, and her eyes moved over his body with curiosity and fascination. He put a hand on her shoulder and urged her to lie back on the bed as he moved over her to rest on his forearms. Damn, she felt good beneath him.

Her breath caught, and her body tensed when his hard manhood pressed against her. He lowered his mouth to hers and kissed her deeply, and she eagerly kissed him back. Her hands were hesitant as they moved over his chest and along his sides to clutch his waist.

Her touch was driving him to the edge. He grabbed her wrists and slammed her hands on the mattress by her head. She let out a startled cry but didn't fight him. His mouth traveled down her neck to her breasts. He pulled a nipple into his mouth and gently teased it.

A breathy moan left her, and her body arched beneath him. Her hips moved against him, and he was lost. Unable to stop himself, he moved over her and thrust hard into her in one swift motion. Her body stiffened, and her scream filled the room. He held himself still, and her inner muscles squeezed his shaft. He groaned and bit down softly on her shoulder, trying to get control of himself.

"You're so damn tight," he ground out.

LaRisa dragged air into her lungs, and her body trembled under him. She shifted her hips to ease the pressure, drawing a ragged groan from Strykes and causing him to push farther into her.

His mouth found hers, and his hands gripped her wrists as he moved within her, drawing out slowly before pushing back into her.

Strykes wanted to go slow, but he couldn't. His desire for her was too great. A spark of fear hit him, and he prayed he wouldn't hurt her, but he couldn't stop. His thrusts quickly grew deep and forceful. He held her wrists pinned down onto the bed as he drove hard inside her. He swore savagely when her hips moved against him, meeting his thrust, and the soft sounds of pleasure she made only drove him on. Her cries and his harsh breathing filled the cabin as he pushed them toward release.

"Strykes," she cried as her body shook.

He kissed her deeply as he shifted over her, his hands on her wrists tightening as he thrust hard again and again. He felt her inner muscles tighten around his shaft, and he groaned out a curse. Jesus, she was close, and it felt like heaven.

"God, LaRisa," he growled as he released her wrists.

His hand moved to her hip, and his fingers dug into her skin as he lunged into her. Her hands gripped his back, clinging desperately to him as her body shook from the intense pleasure she felt. Her fingernails bit into his back, and the sharp pain only drove him on. LaRisa's body arched, and she cried out as her release crashed over her in waves.

Strykes gave his own hoarse cry as he emptied himself inside her. As she took him over the edge with her, his body shuddered, and he braced over her on his forearms, not wanting to crush her with his weight.

Her arms went around him to hold him tight as her body trembled beneath his, and she fought for breath. Strykes slowly withdrew and pushed back inside her, savoring the way her muscles gripped him and pulsed as it drew out his pleasure. He pushed himself deep and held himself there until his breathing eased and the trembling in his body lessened.

"Son of a bitch, LaRisa," he ground out as he fought to get enough air into his lungs.

"Stop," she panted. "Stop swearing at me."

He heard the humor in her voice and lifted his head to look at her. "Sorry." He smiled and kissed her softly. "It was just a little overwhelming."

She smiled back at him and cupped his cheek. "Yes, it was."

He looked down at her flushed face and gave her another smile. Her eyes were hooded and glazed with passion. A tranquil bliss settled in their emerald depths, and for the first time since he had met her, she looked completely at ease. There was no tension, no haunted look, just a peacefulness that he hoped he would get to see every day.

He lifted a hand and stroked her hair from her face. "You're beautiful," he told her softly.

She gave him a shy smile and lowered her lashes. Strykes couldn't keep from kissing that perfect mouth. He kissed her gently for a moment before resting his forehead on hers. He had never felt anything so amazing in his life. She had come to him; she had wanted him to take her, and take her he had. He felt his chest grow tight, and worry hit his gut. He had been too rough with her. Christ, he had held her down and taken her savagely.

"LaRisa." He lifted his head, and she looked at him with those beautiful, trusting eyes. "Did-did I hurt you?" he asked hesitantly.

Her brow puckered at the note of uncertainty in his voice. She felt his energy shift, and it startled her. With their bodies joined, she was tuned to him in a way she didn't understand. A buried pain inside him surfaced and flowed over him in a dark wave. She desperately wanted to take that pain away, but she didn't know how. His pale eyes searched hers, and she saw the worry there.

She gave him a soft smile and reached up to stroke his jaw. "No, you didn't hurt me."

She felt the relief flow over him, and he let out a long breath as he rested his forehead to hers again. The pain she experienced had been brief, but it had also been pleasurable. He had taken her body hard and fast, and she had never felt anything like it. She liked the way his body pressed down on hers, the feel of him between her legs. LaRisa couldn't keep her hands from moving across his hard chest to his shoulders. She liked seeing those wide shoulders above her, the way his chest and arm muscles bunched and moved as he drove hard into her.

A soft sound escaped her as heat rushed over her again at the thoughts she was having about him. She had never dreamed being with a man could be like this. No, not just a man. Strykes. He was rough and dominating, and damn it, she liked it. Another wave of heat washed over her, and she couldn't keep from moving her hips against him. She wanted him to take her again. She wanted him to take her all night.

Strykes had to grit his teeth at the small move she made with her hips. Her hands slid up his chest to caress his jaw as she tipped her face to hesitantly kiss him. Her long legs moved to wrap around his hips as her muscles fluttered around his shaft. The air left him in a rush and his body shuddered.

"Give me more," she breathed against his mouth.

He lifted his head to look at her, and he suddenly couldn't breathe. Her emerald eyes were hungry with desire as she looked into his. He felt the tightness in his chest ease and the worry fade as he looked at her. He gave her a slow smile and gladly obliged her.

Chapter Thirteen

LaRisa rolled over and reached for Strykes. He was gone. Her heart leaped, and she looked around the room. The smell of coffee filled the air, and she smiled. Picking up his extra shirt, she swung it on, not bothering to button it as she stepped out to see him at the stove, naked as the day he was born. She felt her stomach clench as she looked him over. He was magnificent. His body was hard, and the muscles bunched as he moved. She felt her face heat as images of his body over her, inside her, flashed through her mind.

"Good morning," he said with a smile as he turned to her.

"Morning," she said shyly as she lowered her eyes.

He chuckled as he moved toward her. "I don't think my shirt ever looked better," he told her as he pulled her close.

She looked at him and gave him a slight smile. "I don't think my kitchen has ever looked better."

He lowered his head and kissed her softly. Much to his surprise, she wrapped her arms around him and drew him close as she urged him to kiss her deeply. He gladly did so with a groan and absently reached to move the coffeepot from the stove before his hands moved up the shirt to caress her bottom.

Strykes lifted her and carried her back to the bed. He laid her down and covered her body with his. He had to have her again. His need for her was urgent, and he couldn't seem to get enough of her. He felt the familiar fear twist his stomach as he settled between her legs. She eagerly lifted to him, and he plunged deep inside her. She cried out and clung to him as he held himself still inside her.

Jesus, she felt like heaven, and he wanted this feeling every day, every time he saw her. His desire for her was strong, and he knew full well he could never have enough of her. He would become obsessed with her and turn into a bastard.

"Strykes?" Her voice held worry as she looked up at him, her eyes searching his as if trying to read his thoughts.

He had to swallow hard as he looked down into her emerald eyes. He suddenly wanted to confess every horrible thing he had done in his life. Strykes wanted to tell her every fear he had and the bastard he would turn into. He wanted to confess his love for her and the fact that his love could kill her in the end.

Instead, he chose to lower his head and kiss her deeply. He sent up a silent prayer that he could be strong enough to leave her before he killed her.

***

LaRisa came from the bedroom buttoning her bodice, and Strykes enjoyed the beauty of her. He sat at the table drinking coffee and wishing this time with her could be permanent.

"You've put my day behind schedule," she teased as she walked to the door. "I'll gather the eggs and be back."

He grinned at her. "Better get used to it."

Outside, Saber barked. Not a greeting bark, but an agitated and fierce bark.

LaRisa frowned. "Something is wrong."

Strykes lunged to his feet as she opened the door. "Don't!"

He grabbed her and jerked her back and away from the open door. She screamed as bullets dug into the floor of the cabin.

"Son of a bitch," Strykes swore as a bullet crashed through the window.

"Strykes," a man yelled from the direction of the barn.

Strykes felt the blood drain from his face. "Son of a bitch," he said again.

"You know him?" LaRisa asked.

"Yeah, I know him." He turned his head to the broken window. "What the hell do you want, Lucas?"

A laugh floated across the air. "I want you dead, you bastard."

"How did he know you were here?"

He let out a frustrated breath. "When I put Saber out. He must have seen me. They've been moving in, and Saber finally saw them," he said, thankful that the dog had warned them.

"We have to get out of here," she told him and tried to move from his embrace.

"What are you doing?"

"I have a way out." She reached up and touched his face. "Trust me."

More bullets riddled the cabin, and Strykes pulled her close again. His eyes went to her rifle. He released her and picked it up.

"Stay down," he ordered as he put the butt of the rifle to his good shoulder.

LaRisa let loose with a shrill whistle. "Saber!"

Chancing a look out the window, Strykes saw the dog running across the yard. Movement behind the barn caught his eye, and he fired the rifle. Pain went through him at the recoil, but the bullet hit its mark, and the man went down.

Saber rushed into the cabin and went to LaRisa. She was on her knees, hugging the dog tightly. She cried out when a barrage of gunfire sounded outside.

Strykes pressed himself to the cabin wall. None of the bullets hit the cabin. The loud boom of a Sharps rifle echoed, and Strykes knew Jonny was out there. Travis and his men had moved in on Lucas. A gun battle ensued outside, but they were still trapped.

Strykes turned to see LaRisa crawling across the floor to her bedroom, dragging a small canvas bag and canteen with her. "Where're you going? Now isn't the time for a nap."

She looked over her shoulder and smiled at him. "I'm going to change. Can't fight a battle in a dress."

He gave her a small grin. "You're always so practical."

Strykes moved to the open door to chance a look out. He could see none of Lucas's men, nor Travis's, but they were determined to kill each other. Gunfire echoed through the air. His eyes moved to his gun belt draped over the back of the chair. He couldn't get to it without passing by the open door.

"Strykes," LaRisa called from the bedroom. "Bring my rifle and shells and get in here."

Strykes frowned but did as she asked. He dove into the bedroom to see her slip under the bed. He heard her pull up a couple of floorboards, and he slid under the bed to see what she was up to. After she had several boards up and set aside, she slid headfirst under the floor. Saber followed without hesitation.

"Come on," she commanded.

Strykes handed her the rifle and a box of shells before sliding under the cabin as well. His eyes quickly adjusted to the dim light beneath the cabin. She moved up and replaced the floorboards. He watched as she moved to the foundation and removed a wooden panel.

"Stay on your belly and follow the ditch. I'll be right behind you."

He gave her a puzzled look, grabbed the rifle and shells, and crawled along a ditch. He threw a look over his shoulder to see her replace the panel and follow him. The grass around the ditch was tall and gave them excellent cover as they moved along. From the sounds of the gunfire, Travis had Lucas and his bunch busy. With any luck, Lucas wouldn't see them slipping away.

Strykes crawled along until the ditch faced a patch of bushes at the base of the hill behind the cabin. He looked over his shoulder at LaRisa, and she motioned for him to keep going. He slipped under the bushes. On the other side, the ditch ended, and he rolled to the side and waited for LaRisa. She emerged with Saber right behind her. He frowned. She had trained her dog to crawl low as well.

"Saber, you can't come," she said as she cast a look around and stood. "Go." She pointed to the hillside, and the dog took off.

"Where is he going?"

She didn't answer as she moved away. As she walked, she tied the small bag to her belt and slung the canteen over her head and shoulder.

Strykes followed her through the dense trees. There were a hell of a lot of questions he was going to ask her if they lived through this. He followed her to a rock outcrop, and she disappeared. He frowned and hurried after her. She slipped into a crevice between the rocks, and he followed. His large frame almost didn't fit. With some swearing and maneuvering, he made it inside.

"Stay close," she said and took him by the hand.

Strykes went with her, and darkness swallowed them. "Is it too late to tell you I'm afraid of the dark?"

She chuckled. "Yep. Now be quiet."

Strykes felt her place her steps with purpose, and she counted the steps softly as they moved.

He held her hand tightly and stooped over to keep from hitting his head on anything he couldn't see.

LaRisa stopped. "Stay here," she told him and released his hand.

"Not a problem," he grumbled. Just where the hell was he going to go?

"It's here somewhere," she muttered. "Ah, here we are."

Strykes heard her rustling around and wished like hell he could see what she was doing. His wish was granted when there was a spark, and light filled the dark space. He blinked against the glare to see LaRisa standing before him with a torch. He drank in the sight of her. She wore pants and had slipped on his extra shirt. It was far too big, but damn, she looked good in it. Her hair had come loose and hung around her in tangled waves, the torch casting light over the flaming locks.

"Come on. We have to go deeper." She grabbed the extra torch and tinderbox.

Strykes nodded and gripped the rifle tightly before he followed her through the caverns. She led him down a long passageway into a larger room, where she stopped and turned to him.

"We'll take a break here," she said and sat down on a rock. She stabbed the torch in the dirt.

Strykes knelt in the dirt in front of her and took her face in his hands. He kissed her deeply, and she eagerly kissed him back. God, he had been so afraid for her. His hands moved over her body, checking for any damage. When he found her to be unharmed, he drew back and took her hands in his.

"Where the hell are we?" he asked as he glanced around the dim cavern.

LaRisa took a deep breath. "This is a cave."

He shot her a look of impatience. "I know that. Why are we here?"

"We"—she smiled at him—"are saving our ass's."

He quirked an eyebrow at her. "From the looks of things, I'd say you've been planning this for some time."

She shrugged. "When we were kids, we'd explore all through the caves. I'm familiar with them." Before he could ask any more questions, she hurried on. "The caves go through the hill, and there is an opening on the other side. It's close to my parents' house."

"How in the world did you find this place?" he asked. The crack they had crawled through could easily be overlooked. Only people who already knew about it would be able to find it.

"My grandpa and his neighbor found a tunnel and explored. It was on the other side of the hill, and it's a network of tunnels and caves all through the hills," she explained, thinking fondly of the memories. "Each time we explored, we went deeper. Eventually we found a way out on the other side."

He eyed her closely. "And you just happen to have an escape route to the cave from your cabin?"

"Yes." She smiled and stood. "Never know when a gunman will show up with an army after him." She picked up her torch. "We best get moving."

Strykes wanted to ask more but was quiet as he picked up the rifle and box of shells and followed her. He sure as hell didn't want to get lost in this place. He only hoped that LaRisa indeed knew where they were going.

Strykes followed her through the maze of caverns. Occasionally she would stop, find a mark on the stones, and keep going. No doubt she had mapped the way to her parents. How long had she spent exploring the caves? Why did she feel the need to have a secret passage to her parents' house? There was beginning to be far too many questions he needed answers for. He was certain she wouldn't answer them.

Chapter Fourteen

LaRisa slipped through a narrow opening, and Strykes swore as he followed. If these passages got any smaller, he wouldn't fit. He squeezed his way through to see her standing in a large room. Crystals and rock formations glittered in the torchlight, and he took a moment to look around. If men weren't trying to kill him, he would like to look things over more closely. He heard water and saw a small waterfall and a pool below it.

LaRisa gave a heaving sigh. "We'll rest here for a spell."

Strykes turned to see her set the torch to a small pile of wood on the ground in a fire pit, and in no time, flames licked up the dry wood. She put out the torch and turned to him. She looked so beautiful there in the firelight with her hair tangled and her face dirty.

"Come on and get some rest," she said as she moved to a metal box next to the fire pit. "We still have quite a way to go."

"I don't think we should have a fire," he told her. "They could smell the smoke."

She opened the box and pulled out a couple of blankets. She gave them a shake and inspected them. "Good. The mice didn't get to them." She turned to him. "They won't smell the smoke. This cavern has many tunnels above, and the smoke disperses and disappears."

He quirked an eyebrow at her. "Sounds like you've had this escape planned for a long time."

She gave him a nervous smile. "Like I said, we explored a lot. Go wash up in the pool, and we'll get some rest," she told him as she spread the blankets out.

Strykes went to the small pool and splashed the cool water over his face. It felt good, and he squatted there for a long time looking at the water. The pool was small and had no outlet that he could see. The water fell from a small fall from above, and the pool never grew in size. He imagined there was an outlet beneath the rocks and the water flowed to different caves below.

"We can drink it too," she told him as she washed her face and hands. "It tastes terrible, but it won't kill us."

He watched her as she stood and went to the blankets she had laid out. She sat down and pulled off her boots to set them aside. He stood and walked to her as she did her best to manage her hair. There were so many questions rolling through his mind and so many things he didn't understand.

He stepped up to her and knelt on the blanket. "Have campouts too?" He noted her nervous behavior, and he had seen a flicker of fear in her eyes.

"Yes, we did." She took a drink from the canteen and handed it to him.

He took it and drank, keeping his eyes on her. He laid the canteen aside. "You going to tell me the real reason for the mapped path and conveniently placed supplies?"

She looked at him for a long moment. "No" was all she said as she lay back and closed her eyes.

Strykes moved close to her and leaned over her. She stiffened and her eyes flew open. He placed his hands on either side of her, and his pale-blue eyes held hers steadily.

"Tell me, LaRisa." His voice was low. "This has been too well planned. The escape route under your cabin, the ditch behind your house that leads to a well-stocked cave that ends at your parents' house." He leaned over her more. "What are you afraid of?"

She swallowed hard. "Nothing."

His eyes hardened. "I'm not letting this go, LaRisa." The thought of her being afraid and feeling the need to run tore at him. He would kill whoever was trying to hurt her. "Who are you afraid of?"

She bit her lip and appeared to have trouble finding her voice. "You, at the moment."

Strykes blinked at her. Jesus, he could be a bastard. He let out a long breath and rested his forehead against hers. "I don't mean to scare you. I just want you safe," he told her and lifted his head to look at her again. His expression softened.

"I am safe," she told him. "Nobody can find me here."

He reached out and stroked her cheek. "Who can't find you? Who do you want to hide from?"

Tears flooded her eyes. "Everyone."

He gave her a puzzled look. "Why?"

"You wouldn't understand." She turned her face away.

Strykes took her chin and made her look at him. "Try me."

"No." She tried to scoot away, but he lowered his chest to hers, pinning her down. Her tears escaped the corners of her eyes. "I can't tell you."

He cupped her face in his large hand. "LaRisa, please tell me."

"I can't." Her voice was tight, and the tears flowed freely now.

"I'm not giving up on this," he told her flatly.

She blinked her tears away until he came into focus. "And I'm not telling you. If I do, you'll be different toward me." Her heart ached. She would die if he gave her the looks or if she heard him whisper about her.

"LaRisa." He brushed his mouth gently across hers. "Nothing you say could change how I feel about you."

"You say that now," she said, choking back a sob.

He pulled back and looked into her tear filled eyes. "I'll always say that. I'll drop it for now, but you're going to tell me," he said firmly and softly kissed her again. "I care about you, LaRisa," he said against her lips.

LaRisa choked on a sob and put her arms around him. She held him to her as he gently kissed her. He would ask too many questions, and she didn't want to answer them. Would he still care when he found out she was a witch? The thought of him turning his back on her broke her heart. She cared about him too. She liked having him in her life and wasn't ready for that to end. LaRisa was sure this was what love was supposed to be like. Love was a new feeling for her. She liked it.

"Try to get some sleep," he told her as he held her close.

She nodded against his chest and nestled into him.

Strykes felt the tension start to leave LaRisa as they lay there in the weak light of the fire. She shifted closer to him, and he had to stifle a groan. Damn, he wanted her, but they needed to rest.

They lay there for a long time, and he could tell she wasn't sleeping. He understood she feared being chased, but she felt safe in the caves.

"Strykes?" The word was hesitant.

"Yah?"

"What made you leave home?"

He was silent for a long time as the memories came. Memories he had spent years trying to forget. "The Yankees attacked the plantation my family lived on. The plantation owner's son, Mark, and I were best friends. My father worked for his father, and we grew up together. I spent most of my time at his house, and his parents treated me like I was one of their own.

"Then a group of Jayhawkers came. It seems that Mark's father had been supplying Confederate troops with rifles and horses. They hung him, right there in front of his wife and daughters. Then they burned the place to the ground."

"And they killed Mark?" she asked tentatively.

"No. He made it to our place, and we lit out together. I sent my sisters to live with an aunt, and we took off. We met up with a group of Missouri militia and joined them. Our group was hiding at a farmer's place a few months later. Mark was to go out on guard duty. When he opened the door, a group of Yanks hiding in the trees shot him."

She nestled into him and hugged him to her. "I'm sorry."

"I pulled him back through the door. He had been shot full of holes. It seemed like it took him forever to die, though it was only a few minutes. There was nothing I could do to save him. All I could do was hold him and be there for him. And then he was dead. I could've prevented it, but it had happened anyway."

"What could you have done?" she asked softly.

"I could've gone on guard duty instead. We drew straws as a joke, and he drew the short one. It got him killed. Those of us that weren't dead had to run like hell to get out of there. When I looked back, they had set fire to the house, and Mark's body went with it."

The silence stretched out in the small cavern before she spoke. "Where are your sisters now?"

He shrugged. "New Orleans, as far as I know. Get some sleep. Tomorrow's going to be a long day."

Strykes lay looking up at the dark ceiling of the cave as he held LaRisa to him. Memories of his past flooded him. There had been so much blood and death in his life. He desperately wanted that to change. Foolishly, he had thought Rimrock would be the place to start over, but his past had caught up to him, and the killing would continue.

"Strykes?"

Her sleepy voice gave him a start. "Huh?"

"What is your first name?"

He said nothing for a time, realizing that probably nobody in town knew his full name. It wasn't something he had ever bothered to clear up. Nobody had called him by it for so many years that he never gave it much thought.

"Well?" she prodded when she didn't receive an answer.

"Uh, it's Bret."

She made a noise of approval. "Bret."

It came off her tongue like a heated whisper, and the sound sent a warm jolt through his body. Then she sighed, and he knew she was asleep. He pulled her tighter against him and savored the feel of her. He was pretty damn sure he was hopelessly in love with her, and he would do anything to protect her.

His heart twisted. But who would protect her from him? He tried to push away his fear as he held her close. Love turned to obsession. Obsession turned to complete control. And complete control turned to murder. That was how it went, if he remembered correctly.

Chapter Fifteen

LaRisa woke with a groan. Sleeping on the hard, lumpy ground had caused her muscles to protest her movement. Carefully, she drew away from Strykes and added more wood to the dying embers. After a moment, she had a tiny fire going again. She sat there and let the small flames warm her body.

She wasn't sure how long they had slept, but she knew they had several hours of hard climbing ahead of them. The path to her parents' house wasn't easy in places. LaRisa looked at Strykes as he slept. The climbing would rip open his shoulder again and ruin all the healing that had occurred. He would be in pain and not be able to move fast when he needed to.

Quietly, she moved to where he slept. She bit down on her bottom lip and leaned over him. Carefully, she undid the button of his shirt and slid her hand beneath it. She rested her palm over the wound on his shoulder and closed her eyes. The energy flowed into her hand. She bit harder on her lip as her palm heated. She would heal it enough to keep him from bleeding anymore and hurting too badly.

"LaRisa?" Strykes reached out and grabbed her wrist.

Her eyes flew open, and she cried out. She felt the energy shift at her surge of fear. Jesus, she would kill him. She tried desperately to pull free from his grasp. He held tight, and she balled her hand into a fist and tried to turn her palm from his skin. She had to break the touch before she hurt him. The energy was shifting; she could feel it. The heel of her hand was still against his skin. She struggled to free herself from his iron hold.

"Strykes, let me go," she begged.

"What's wrong?" he asked. She looked totally terrified. He opened his mouth to say something and stopped. His heart surged in his chest, and a tight pressure began to squeeze. "Jesus." He groaned against the pain in his chest.

"Please!" she cried as tears ran down her cheeks. She could feel herself drawing his energy. "You have to let me go. Now!" she sobbed as she pulled at her arm.

Strykes released her and felt the pressure in his chest ease. She scrambled away from him. She turned her back to him and buried her face in her hands. Her shoulders shook as she silently sobbed. Strykes sat up with a hand over his heart. It began to beat normally again, and the pain was gone. What the hell had happened? His hand went to his shoulder to find the skin was hot to the touch. He moved his fingers over the bullet wound. It was barely there. He turned and examined it in the dim firelight to see only a pink mark remaining.

His eyes shot to LaRisa. Her body trembled, and her tangled hair covered her face. "LaRisa?" He moved up behind her. He reached up and placed a hand on her shoulder. She flinched away, and he moved around to face her. "LaRisa, look at me."

She still held her hands over her face and turned from him. She couldn't look at him. He had seen what she had done. She was afraid of what she would see in his eyes. If he had only known how close he had been to death. Another sob escaped her at the thought of accidentally killing him.

"LaRisa, damn it." He grabbed her shoulders. "Look at me."

She shrank away from him and tried to break his hold. Fisting her hands, she pulled them close to her chest, not wanting to touch him. She turned her face from him and kept her eyes closed. Nausea washed over her. The energy overload was setting in.

"I'm going to be sick," she said as she struggled to get out of his grasp.

Strykes released her, and she scrambled away. She knelt in the dirt and emptied her stomach onto the ground. He grabbed the canteen and knelt behind her. He gathered her hair in his hands and waited for her to finish.

He drew her back against him and held her close as he bathed her face with the wet handkerchief. Her body trembled as he held her; her breathing was ragged. What in the hell had happened? He held her to him until her trembling eased and her breathing returned to normal.

"LaRisa," he whispered against her ear. "Talk to me, honey."

She whimpered and tried to move away. He tightened his hold on her and turned her enough to see her face. She tried to turn from him, but his hand cupped her cheek and held her still. Her eyes were still closed, and tears spilled down her cheeks.

"Look at me," he demanded softly.

Her stomach knotted with dread, and slowly she opened her eyes. She was so afraid of what she would see. New tears rolled down her cheeks as she looked into his eyes. She didn't see fear or accusation or even disbelief. She only saw caring and compassion on his worried face. Didn't he realize what had just happened? He was so calm and concerned for her that it tore at her heart.

His hand stroked her cheek. "Are you all right now?"

She could only nod. How could she explain how she felt to him? So many emotions and feelings crashed over her, she didn't know if she would ever get them sorted out.

"What just happened, LaRisa?" he asked softly. He saw the fear flicker in her eyes, and she tried to pull away. "No." He tightened his hold on her. "You're going to talk to me."

Panic threatened to choke her. "I can't."

"After what just happened, you had better," he informed her. "What did you do to my shoulder?"

"Strykes, please," she sobbed. "Don't make me."

Strykes swore and pulled her to the blankets. He sat down, pulling her across his lap as he wrapped the other blanket around her. She buried her face in his neck and still had her hands balled up as if she were afraid to touch him.

"How did you fix my shoulder?" he asked quietly.

"We should probably get going," she ventured, hoping he would drop the subject.

"Not until you answer me," he told her.

"No," she whimpered.

"You healed my shoulder. Tell me how."

She swallowed hard, knowing she would have to tell him everything. "I touched you."

Confusion and disbelief filled his eyes. "Your touch healed me?"

She nodded. "I can't explain it. It's just something I can do. I have a special kind of energy inside me, and I can heal wounds."

He was silent for a moment. "If you can heal, why didn't you do it sooner?"

She sighed. "I did. You had a bullet hole through your leg, and I healed it. And when I took the bullet out of your shoulder, I couldn't stop the bleeding. I healed it enough to stop the bleeding. I couldn't heal it all the way." She didn't tell him it was because she was about to kill him.

"Why did you choose to finish healing it now?"

"I had to. I was worried you might hurt your shoulder when we climb the rocks," she said as tears rolled down her cheeks. "I just wanted to heal you a little."

He looked down at the wound, which was all but gone. "But you healed it more than you wanted."

She nodded. "I can't control it very well because I don't do it often. It's not something I like to do."

"You've done this before?"

She swallowed hard. "A couple times." She would tell him no more.

"When I woke up, what happened?"

She choked on a sob. "You weren't supposed to wake up. You scared me, and I could have…" Her voice broke off as she cried.

He held her close. "I didn't mean to scare you. Your hand was so damn hot, I thought you were burning me."

"Why would I burn you?" she snapped.

He gave a low chuckle. "I don't know, but that was the only thing I could relate to the heat." He smoothed her hair back. "Do you always get sick after?"

"No. I usually just faint," she said simply.

"Why was this time different?"

She shrugged. If he didn't suspect anything, she sure as hell wasn't going to tell him she could have killed him. "Because I was scared" was all she offered. "I didn't want this." She looked at her hands as new tears rolled down her cheeks. "I'm not a witch."

He wiped at her tears with his thumbs. "I know. You just have a special gift."

"Now you'll be different to me since you know." Her voice was tight.

"No." He met her tear-filled eyes steadily. "I won't be different. I may be confused as hell, but I care about you, and nothing will change that."

She let out a whimper and closed her eyes. Relief washed over her, and she felt completely drained. He still cared, even after all that had happened. He knew, and he didn't mind. But he didn't know she had almost killed him either.

"We'll talk about this more," he informed her. "Preferably when people aren't trying to kill us."

She lifted her eyes to his, and he swore at the raw emotion reflected there. Lowering his lips to hers, he softly kissed her mouth. He groaned as he felt himself harden. He wanted her, but now was not the time. Pulling back, he brushed his knuckles along her cheek.

"Can you eat something?"

LaRisa nodded. "I think so."

Strykes moved her from his lap and turned to get the small bag she had brought. He handed it to her and watched her dig out a piece of jerky and eat. He rolled his wounded shoulder and felt no pain. She had healed him. It was impossible, but she had done it.

"When did you discover you had this ability?"

She stilled in the act of taking another bite, no doubt thinking about how much she wanted to tell him. Strykes waited patiently.

"It was something that I knew would happen to me." She finished with the jerky and focused on managing her tangled hair.

"Why is that?"

"Because it runs in my family. The women in my family are…" She struggled to find the right word. "Different. Many would call us witches. Family stories tell that some of our relatives many years ago were burned for being witches."

Strykes nodded as he thought. "That's why you don't like going to town and why people treat you differently."

She nodded and finally met his eyes. "Yes. That is why I have a path through the caves."

"And you trained Saber to escape with you."

"I was afraid someone might hurt him if they couldn't get me, so he knows to come with me. He can't climb through the caves, so he knows to go to my parents' place and wait for me. It's the only place I can be truly safe."

Strykes felt a pang in his chest at the misery in her voice. She didn't protest as he took her in his arms and held her close. Her arms went around him, and she buried her face in his chest.

"You're safe, LaRisa. I'll keep you safe."

He hoped it wasn't a lie. He could keep her safe from the world, but who would keep her safe from him when the time came?

***

Strykes wasn't sure how long they had been making their way through the caves. With no sun to gauge time, they could have been wandering around for minutes or hours. It was slow progress in many places, as they had to scale rocks and crawl on hands and knees in places.

"Here's the hard part," she told him and held up the torch.

Strykes swore as he looked up. A huge rock a good thirty feet tall loomed over them. The rock had split down the center, leaving it in two halves, separated by a wide crack. How the hell did she plan on climbing that? He watched as she moved to stand between the rocks.

"Just do like I do," she told him as she reached a foot up to wedge into a hollowed-out place in the rock. "We carved a ladder of sorts when we were kids." She let out a soft laugh. "It took a long time."

Strykes watched as she raised a hand and placed it in another carved-out notch before lifting her other foot to wedge into another notch. She looked at him, and he gave her a nod, understanding the method of climbing. He stepped forward and kissed her. She was eye level with him as she hung between the rocks. She made no protest as she kissed him back.

"Be careful," he told her as he drew back.

"I've done this several times before," she told him with a smile.

He secured the rifle in his belt behind his back and took the torch from her. "I'll take this, so you have both hands to climb with."

The going was difficult, and Strykes was grateful that LaRisa had healed his shoulder. By the time they reached the top, they were both breathing hard, and their muscles trembled from the exertion. They took several moments to sit at the top and catch their breath.

"It's not much farther," she told him as she stood, taking the torch from him.

"Glad to hear it," he grumbled as he got to his feet and followed her.

LaRisa led him through several passages, and after a while, he felt air rush over his skin. They were getting close to the outside world. Soon there was a small breeze, and the passageway walls were easier to see.

"Almost out," LaRisa said as she put out the torch and laid it and the tinderbox on a rock outcrop.

Taking his hand, she led him the way out into the sunlight. Strykes stood there for a moment, savoring the feel of the wind swirling around him. The sun was dipping over the horizon, indicating that they had been in the cave a day and a half.

"Come on," she said as she released his hand and led the way through the trees. "We have to cross the river. There is a small bridge near here."

Strykes followed a few paces behind her. What would happen now? Had Travis killed Lucas? He wouldn't know until he got back to town. But if Lucas was still alive, getting to town alive might prove difficult.

His eyes focused on LaRisa. What would happen between them now? The best thing for her was for him to ride away and never look back. But now that he had a taste of her passion, he feared that leaving her would be impossible.

Being so lost in his thoughts, Strykes didn't see the men waiting for them until it was too late.

Chapter Sixteen

Without warning, a man darted from behind a group of trees and grabbed LaRisa. She screamed and tried to fight him, but the man slid his arm across her throat and put pressure on it.

Strykes instantly had the rifle to his shoulder. Two men came at him from the concealment of the brush, and he turned the rifle on them, shooting one man in the chest. The other man shoved the rifle away and landed a solid punch to Strykes's stomach. He doubled over, using the move to bring the rifle butt down into the man's knee. The man howled in pain, and Strykes turned the rifle and shot him in the throat.

His attention went back to the man holding LaRisa as he aimed the rifle at his forehead. "Let her go."

"Not a chance, Strykes."

Recognition hit him. "Martin. You son of a bitch."

"It's nice to see you too. Lucas will be glad to know I found you."

"Where is he?"

"Someplace your marshal friend would never look. He's waiting for you."

"How did you find us?" Strykes demanded. He had to get Martin talking and buy himself time to figure out a way to get LaRisa away from him.

"We followed that dog of hers," he said triumphantly. "Lucas saw him on the hill behind the cabin. He didn't come out the front door, so that meant there was a back way out. That marshal forced us to scatter and run. Lucas and us broke off and came after the dog. He came straight to this place and stayed for a while before he headed off to that ranch over there." He jerked his head, showing the direction of the ranch. "And Lucas had us hang around and keep an eye out for the two of you."

"Where is Lucas now?" Strykes demanded as he contemplated taking the shot, but LaRisa was too close to risk it.

"You know Lucas, he always sets up a place to regroup. If I don't kill you, I'll take you to him."

LaRisa's eyes were wide as she watched Strykes face off with the man. He held her tightly against him, his arm across her throat. She could hardly breathe, and the fear overwhelmed her.

Martin had his pistol pointed directly at Strykes. And though she knew Strykes was aiming at the man, the rifle looked like it was aimed at her. She knew Strykes was an excellent shot, but she wasn't so sure how his aim was left-handed.

"Let her go, Martin," Strykes told him. "You came after me, not her. She has nothing to do with this."

Martin smiled at him. "Oh, I think she does. I can use her to keep you in line."

"Let her go, and I'll come with you."

"Throw the rifle down," he ordered. "Then she goes free."

Strykes hesitated a long time, then the rifle lowered, and he let it fall to the ground. "Let her go."

"Lucas wanted you alive, but this is mighty tempting," he said with a grin. "I always wanted to prove myself better than you."

Strykes glared at him. "Then let her go and give me a pistol."

"I don't think so," he said and leveled his pistol at Strykes's chest.

LaRisa cried out in fear, and her heart pounded. He was going to kill Strykes. No, this couldn't happen. She clamped both her hands on Martin's forearm across her neck. She closed her eyes and reached for the energy. Her hands heated, and his energy crashed into her.

"What the hell?" Martin gasped, the pistol wavering.

Strykes watched as Martin's eyes went wide and the pistol fell to the ground. Martin gasped for breath, his free hand going to his chest. He went to his knees, dragging LaRisa down with him. Her hands clung to his arm as they went to the ground. Martin's breath was ragged, and he wheezed as he fought for air. His hand clutched at his chest. He tried to shove LaRisa away, but she hung on. His body toppled over, and he convulsed on the ground.

Strykes rushed to LaRisa and pulled her away from the man. Martin was no longer moving. His skin was pale, and his dead eyes stared at the sky. LaRisa shook uncontrollably. Her hands were fists tucked close to her body. She knelt on the ground, dragging air into her lungs. Her body was on fire. Her skin was so hot against his hands.

He felt her fill her lungs, and his hand clamped over her mouth to muffle the scream that erupted from her. It was a long, agonized scream, and when she had finished, she filled her lungs and did it again. His stomach was in a tight knot, and his heart pounded. What the hell was happening? What had happened to Martin? He looked at the man's body. One minute he had been going to shoot Strykes, the next he was dead.

Finally, LaRisa stopped screaming. He slowly lowered his hand from her mouth and let her gasp in air. Her body shook violently, and she was so damn hot to touch. Suddenly, she threw herself to the side and emptied her stomach. She heaved for a long time. Strykes caught her before she collapsed to the ground.

"LaRisa." Strykes held her close and pushed her hair from her face. "What's wrong?" He felt so helpless, and it was a feeling he didn't like.

In the fading light, her eyes looked foggy. They stared unseeing at him. It felt as if her body was heating even more. The shaking was uncontrollable. He swore when he saw blood leaking from her nose.

"It's so hot." Her voice was barely a whisper. "Bret, I—" Her voice broke off as her body convulsed.

Strykes swore and picked her up in his arms. He hurried down the hill and ran the distance to the river. He had to get her cooled off fast. Wading into the river until he was waist deep, he sank to his knees in the water. She gave a startled gasp as the cold water washed over her. Her arms went around his neck, and she clung to him. He used his hands to cup water and pour it over her head and on her neck.

"I know it's cold, honey," he soothed as he washed water over her. "We have to get you cooled off."

After what seemed like an eternity, her body cooled. She sagged against him, her body going limp. He pulled back and looked at her face. Her eyes were open yet still foggy and unseeing.

"LaRisa, I need you to tell me the direction to your parents' house," he told her. He wasn't sure of the right direction and didn't want her passing out before he knew where to take her. Her eyes rolled, and he shook her. "Stay with me, honey."

She whimpered and tried to look at him.

"Which way?"

She heard his voice from far off. "East," she whispered. "G-go east." Her eyes wouldn't focus, and she couldn't see Strykes, though she knew he was there. "Up over th-the hill."

Strykes held her tightly to him and left the river. He hurried up the hill, and at the top, he stopped to survey the darkness below. In the distance, he could make out the dark shapes of buildings, and a faint light glowed in the house.

"LaRisa, you still with me?" he asked against her hair.

She let out a soft moan and went completely limp in his arms. Jesus, he had to get her help. He didn't know what the hell was wrong with her, and it scared him. Strykes ran the distance to the house. His body ached and his lungs burned, but he had to get her to her parents. They might know what to do for her.

A couple of dogs set into barking as he neared the house. He recognized one as Saber. He spoke to the dog, and he went quiet, trotting along with him as he approached the house. The door opened as he climbed the steps.

Matthew Reeves stood there at the open door. He took in Strykes, breathing hard, and LaRisa in his arms. His face paled, and he moved aside to let him in.

"Follow me," he told Strykes and led him through the house. "Shyfawn!" he called as he headed for the stairs.

Shyfawn came from the kitchen. "What is it?" she asked, then saw her daughter. "LaRisa." She rushed up the stairs behind Strykes.

Matthew opened a door and went in. "Lay her here." He gestured to the bed.

Strykes laid her down and stepped back. Shyfawn was at her side in an instant. He watched as she checked her daughter over.

"What happened?" she asked Strykes.

Strykes tried to calm his breathing. "I don't know. We were ambushed at her cabin and made our way here through the caverns." He took another deep breath. "We ran into a couple men at the river, and one had a hold of her." He wasn't sure how to explain the rest. "Then he died, and she got sick."

Shyfawn gasped and looked at Matthew. "No." Her eyes went to Strykes. "How did he die?"

Strykes shook his head. "I'm not sure. It was like his heart gave out."

"Oh God," she breathed, and her hands moved over LaRisa. "She's so warm," she muttered.

"She was burning up, and I dunked her in the river. It seemed to help some," Strykes explained.

Shyfawn wiped at the blood smeared on her face. "Did he hurt her?"

"No. Her nose started to bleed. I'm not sure why it happened."

"Can you do anything for her?" Matthew asked.

Shyfawn looked at him helplessly. "I don't know. There's no physical wound. I'm not sure I can help her."

Matthew had to clear his throat. "Can you try?"

Tears well in Shyfawn's eyes, and she looked at Strykes for a moment. "Can you step out for a moment?"

"You can do it too?" he asked, knowing what Shyfawn would do. "I know about her. She healed me."

Shyfawn looked at Matthew, and he nodded. She turned her attention to LaRisa and placed a hand on her forehead and another over her heart. She closed her eyes and let the energy flow. There was no wound to heal, and she wasn't sure what to do. She sent the energy deeper into her daughter. A blast of agony slammed into Shyfawn, and she cried out, jerking away from LaRisa. Matthew was beside her in an instant.

"Shyfawn, what is it?" He pulled her into his arms.

"She's in so much pain," Shyfawn cried against his shoulder.

Strykes stepped up to the bed. "How? She's not wounded."

Shyfawn turned tear-filled eyes to him. "On the inside. She is full of pain." She rested her cheek against Matthew's chest. "LaRisa will be fine. She just needs rest and time to let the energy disperse."

Strykes gave her a puzzled look. "Energy?"

Shyfawn sighed. "It takes energy for us to do what we do. Right now, she has too much."

He looked at LaRisa. He had no idea what Shyfawn was talking about. How could someone have too much energy? His mind went over and over the ordeal with Martin. LaRisa had a tight hold on him when he fell. Strykes's hand absently moved to his shoulder. If she used her hands to heal him, was it possible she used her hands to kill Martin? Jesus, the realization hit him full force. She had taken Martin's energy. She had killed the man to save Strykes.

Strykes looked at Shyfawn. She nodded as if reading the question there. He swore and sat on the bed next to LaRisa. She had killed for him and was in a deep pain he couldn't imagine.

"Strykes, you look exhausted," Shyfawn said as she wiped at her tears. "I'll fix you something to eat before you sleep. We'll get your clothes dry, and you can stay in the spare room."

He nodded absently. "That would be fine." He brushed LaRisa's hair from her forehead.

She murmured his name and rolled over to reach for him. Her hand rested on his thigh, and he placed his over the top of hers. Her fingers lifted to lace with his. He could feel her body was much cooler than before. Relief flowed over him to know she would be all right.

He had to clear his throat before he spoke. "She'll need to eat. She got very sick and will be starving when she wakes up."

"I'll fix her something as well."

Something in Shyfawn's voice made him look at her. Her eyes were swimming with tears, and she only nodded. Matthew walked with her out of the room.

When the door was closed, Strykes lay beside LaRisa and pulled her close, placing a kiss on her forehead. She nestled against him and let out a contented sigh. He held her for a long time before he began removing her wet clothes. Her father would probably kill him for doing this, but he didn't give a damn.

***

In the dining room, Matthew sat at the table and pulled Shyfawn across his lap to hold her close. "She'll be fine."

Shyfawn nodded and ran her hand along Matthew's jaw. "I know. I just don't like knowing the pain she's in. She killed someone, and she is hurting over it. Not just from the energy overload, but she's devastated for having to kill him." Tears ran down her cheeks.

"We'll help her get through it," Matthew told her as he wiped at her tears.

"I don't think it's us she needs."

His brow puckered. "What do you mean?"

"Strykes," she said softly and felt Matthew stiffen. "She touched him, Matthew." Fresh tears filled her eyes. "LaRisa never touches anyone, not even us. She reached out for him."

Matthew nodded. She was right; LaRisa never touched people. Why did it have to be Strykes?

***

Strykes entered the dining room. Shyfawn turned tearful eyes to him, and Matthew shot him the hard look of a protective father.

"She's sleeping," he told them.

"Have a seat," Shyfawn told him before disappearing into the kitchen. She returned shortly later with a plate of food to set on the table.

Strykes couldn't stop the tired groan that escaped him as he sat in the chair. "Thank you," he said as he looked his plate over.

She smiled. "I thought you'd be hungry."

He nodded and met Shyfawn's eyes evenly. "Before I dig in, please tell me what's going on. I've seen it and I've felt it, but I don't understand it."

Shyfawn looked at her husband, then back at Strykes. "You say she healed you."

"Yes." He picked up his fork and poked at the food before him. "We were in the caverns resting, and I fell asleep. I woke up to a fire burning my shoulder. LaRisa had her hand over the gunshot wound."

"She tried to heal you?" Shyfawn asked.

"She *did* heal me. There is no wound at all. I was startled and grabbed her wrist. She became scared and tried to get me to let her go. I wouldn't, and she seemed to panic."

Shyfawn chewed at her thumbnail. "Was she still touching you?"

He nodded. "She was trying not to, though."

"She was scared. And how did you feel?" she asked.

"You want to know if my heart went crazy and I couldn't breathe?" He nodded. "Yes, I felt like a giant fist was squeezing my chest."

She sighed and once again sat on Matthew's lap. She settled against her husband as he held her. "LaRisa can't control her gift. She hasn't used it much and is unsure of her ability. She's had to use it in emergencies, but once when she was young, things went wrong."

"Wrong?" Strykes asked, his eyes holding steady on Shyfawn.

She took a deep breath. "I won't give all the details. If LaRisa wants you to know, she will tell you. She was thirteen, and Doc Sam's father had been shot. LaRisa tried to help him, but she was so scared that the energy didn't flow like it should. Cal died, and LaRisa was devastated."

"Did she react the same way as tonight?" he asked.

She nodded. "Yes. Her body raged with fever, and she became very ill."

"Her eyes." Strykes fought a shudder at remembering her eyes. "They were glazed, almost foggy, and she couldn't see."

"Yes. I don't know how it happens, but the consequences are severe." Her hand gripped Matthew's. "This time was worse, I think, because she purposely took his life. She completely drained him to save you, and the backlash is hurting her."

Strykes nodded. "Yeah, he had a gun on me and was going to kill me. She didn't let that happen." He thought for a moment. "Is that why she wears gloves in town?"

Shyfawn nodded. "She's so afraid she'll hurt someone."

Strykes grunted as he thought. "A lot of things make sense now."

"I'll bet," Matthew grumbled.

Strykes didn't miss the edge in his voice. He shot the man a hard look. "Don't you think if I tried to hurt her, I'd be dead? She doesn't need a gun to kill me."

"Strykes, you need to eat and get some rest."

He nodded but didn't eat. "Can you take lives?"

Shyfawn shook her head. "No, I can't. And as far as I know, no woman in our family history has ever been able to. I wish every day that my daughter had been spared this. It's a burden she will carry for the rest of her life."

Strykes decided he had prodded into the subject far enough and ate. He knew this had to be hard on Shyfawn, watching her daughter suffer and knowing there was nothing she could do to help her. Tomorrow, when LaRisa woke, they would talk about what had happened. Many things were clearer now about her behavior and her fear of being hunted as a witch. But he still had a hell of a lot of questions.

Chapter Seventeen

LaRisa stirred in the soft bed, and she couldn't keep from groaning. Why did she feel like she had been hit by a train? She rolled over and reached for Strykes. She found the bed empty. With a frown, she blinked her eyes open. When they focused, she could see she wasn't in her cabin. She was in her old room at her parents' house.

"LaRisa?" a man said softly from the door.

"Tim?"

LaRisa sat up and turned to see her older brother standing in the doorway. He gave her a smile before he entered and sat on the edge of the bed. His dark-blue eyes couldn't hide the worry he was feeling.

"I'm fine," she assured him.

"I got here as soon as I could," he told her. "Pa sent word that you were in trouble."

"It's over now. We escaped, and I'm safe."

"What possessed you to let a man like Strykes into your cabin?"

She frowned at him. "He needed help."

"And he nearly got you killed."

"I was never close to being killed." She tried not to think of when Martin had her. "I'm fine."

"I told you that you shouldn't be out on your own," he scolded her. "You need to be here."

"Stop being a big brother. I can't live here forever. You left home too," she pointed out.

"That's different. I set up a place to the south to help watch the cattle. This is a big ranch with a lot of stock."

"I know." She gave him a small smile. "I'm glad you're here."

"Not for long. Pa is sending me after Travis."

"Breakfast," Shyfawn announced as she entered the room. "I'm glad you're awake."

"I best get going," Tim said as he stood and walked to the door. "Get some more rest. You look like you need it," he told LaRisa before he left.

LaRisa sighed. "He was always so elegant with words."

Shyfawn laughed. "Just like your father." She placed the tray of food on the dresser before sitting on the bed beside her daughter. "You had us worried when Strykes brought you here," Shyfawn said softly.

Images flashed behind her eyes—escaping her cabin, the caverns, healing and almost hurting Strykes, the trees, and three men with guns. Her heart dropped. She had killed the one called Martin. Taking his life to protect Strykes. Her stomach rolled, and tears burned her eyes.

"I killed someone, Mama," she sobbed and tucked her hands in against her stomach.

Tears filled Shyfawn's emerald eyes. "It's all right, honey. You did what you had to do to survive."

She sobbed and leaned into her mother. Shyfawn held her close as LaRisa leaned her forehead to her shoulder, careful to keep her hands hidden. Shyfawn smoothed her hair back and did her best to comfort her daughter.

"Strykes saw, Mama," she choked out. "He caught me healing him and knows I'm a witch."

"You're no more witch than I am," Shyfawn told her softly but firmly.

Sobs shook her body. "I got scared and almost killed him. I would never forgive myself if that happened."

"But he's alive and healed," she said gently.

"He saw me," she cried. "He saw me kill that man. He's going to be afraid to come near me now."

"Somehow I doubt that." Strykes's deep drawl came from the doorway.

LaRisa gasped, and her head snapped up. She drank in the sight of him as he stood in the doorway, arms folded, leaning a shoulder on the doorframe. He had heard everything. His image blurred as new tears fell. She was aware of him crossing the room to the other side of the bed and felt the mattress give under his weight. She felt her mother move away and stand.

"LaRisa." His hand cupped her cheek to turn her face to him. "Your mother is right. We do what we have to do to survive." His voice was soft. "You did what you had to do."

"But you saw me kill him," she said.

He nodded and wiped at her tears. "And you saw me kill the other two."

"But you were protecting me."

"And *you* were protecting me," he told her gently. "It's no different."

She raised a shaky hand to cover his on her cheek. "Aren't you afraid of me now?"

He took her hand in his and brought her palm to his mouth. "No." He kissed her palm softly.

"How?" Her voice was trembling. "You've seen what I can do."

He laced his fingers through hers and kissed the back of her hand. "LaRisa, if you knew about half the things I've done, you'd be afraid of me. I've done a lot of things I'm ashamed of, and most of it would horrify you."

She reached out with her other hand and ran her fingers across the whiskers on his jaw. "I don't believe you."

"You'd be surprised." He leaned forward and brushed his lips over hers.

They were too lost in each other. Neither saw the tears on Shyfawn's cheeks as she closed the door behind her.

***

Strykes was in the barn helping Matthew repair a stall gate when the sound of approaching horses reached their ears. They stopped work and went to the door to step outside. Four riders were coming toward the ranch. Strykes recognized the marshal's gray horse and Boone's blue roan immediately.

"Looks like Tim is back with Travis," Matthew said simply as they waited for the riders to approach.

Strykes nodded. Matthew had sent his son to town that morning to fetch the marshal. Tim looked much like his father: dark-blue eyes, brown hair, and a strong build. And from the look he cast Strykes that morning before leaving for town, Tim didn't like him any more than Matthew did.

"Afternoon, Travis," Matthew greeted. "I see you brought Boone and Winky with you."

Deputy Heck Tennison laughed as he dismounted. "Someone has to watch his back." He gestured to his one good eye, the other covered by a patch.

Travis dismounted and gave Strykes the once over. "Well, if I told you I was glad to see you still alive, I'd be lying."

Strykes grinned. "I'm happy to disappoint you."

After the fight with Brown had been settled, Boone and Strykes had gone free. Thankfully, the marshal had no evidence to tie either man to anything illegal. Since then, the marshal had settled into a begrudging truce with them.

Boone and Tim dismounted, and Tim took the men's horses into the barn to care for them. Apparently, they intended to stay for a little while.

Strykes looked at Boone. "Is Lucas dead?"

Boone shook his head. "No, we got several of them when they raided LaRisa's, but unfortunately Lucas wasn't one of them."

"Damn," Strykes grumbled, though he had suspected as much.

"And that means the bastard will come after you again," Travis bit out. "I don't know why you gunfighters have to come settle in my town."

Heck chuckled. "But you never hesitate to use Quinn and Jonny when you need help."

"That's different." He turned his attention to Matthew. "I hate to do this to you, Matt, but I need Strykes to stay here."

Matthew shot Strykes a glare before he turned it onto the marshal. "I don't want him here. He'll bring that outlaw down on us."

"That's my point. I have no doubt that Lucas knows he's here. Tim said that Strykes and LaRisa were attacked on their way here. When those men don't return, Lucas will figure out why." Travis's gaze was level and held no room for argument. "He stays here."

"I don't like it."

"We didn't think you would," Heck put in. "Jonny and Quinn are going to help."

"And I'll be here the entire time," Boone told Matthew before he looked at Strykes. "I want him dead too."

Strykes dared a look at Matthew to find the man's eyes shooting daggers at him. He hoped that Travis's plan would work and that it would be over quickly. He had a feeling if Lucas didn't kill him, Matthew would. He had better make sure that none of Matthew's family was hurt in this fight, or he would be a dead man.

***

After three days of nothing, Strykes was getting irritable. He had stayed on lookout in the

175

barn loft with a borrowed rifle and pistol. Lucas hadn't made a move against him yet, and he was getting impatient. Of course, two days of spring rain had probably stopped any plan Lucas might have had. But he cursed the mud as he slopped through it from the barn toward the house.

Matthew had insisted he sleep in the barn, and Strykes couldn't blame him. He wouldn't want an outlaw near his daughter if he had one. But this morning he was anxious to see LaRisa and had headed to the house before the breakfast bell. After a cold night in the barn, he craved a hot cup of coffee. After several nights alone, he craved LaRisa.

Strykes leaped up the steps, scraped mud from his boots on the iron boot scraper, and went inside. He paused inside the front door and listened. A smile crept over his mouth when he heard LaRisa's soft singing. It was a low, haunting melody.

As he moved through the house, he heard another voice blend with hers. Shyfawn. The two singing together sent a shiver down his spine. It was a beautiful sound.

He stopped at the kitchen door to listen to them. They stood at the counter together. LaRisa was cooking at the stove, and Shyfawn was kneading dough. He rested an arm against the doorframe and listened to the haunting Irish ballad. Each sang beautifully on her own, but when their voices blended, it was hypnotic. Strykes could only stand there and watch LaRisa as he listened to the song.

Strykes jumped and his hand flashed for his pistol when he felt a hand on his shoulder. Turning, he saw Matthew standing beside him. He moved his hand from his gun and relaxed. He could tell Matthew didn't like the way he was looking at his daughter, but Strykes didn't really give a damn. LaRisa was special to him.

Matthew gave him a slight smile and turned to watch his wife and daughter as they sang together. It had been a long time since he had heard them sing together, and he let the memories wash over him. LaRisa had always been happy and loved to sing with her mother. But after the day she had taken a life while trying to heal, she had changed. She never smiled, never sang, and had distanced herself from her family. To see LaRisa and Shyfawn together again was a blessing. His daughter was changing, and much to his dismay, he had a feeling it was because of Strykes.

The door opened, and both men turned to see Boone and Tim enter the house. Boone greeted them, and Tim shot Strykes a hard look. The man had been cold toward him since his arrival, and Strykes understood. He had nearly gotten LaRisa killed, and now he was bringing trouble down on the Reeves household.

"Breakfast smells good," Boone said as he stood in the dining room, taking a deep sniff of the air.

LaRisa made her way past the men, carrying two plates filled with pancakes. "Tim, ring the bell for breakfast." On her return trip to the kitchen, she smiled at Strykes and let her hand brush across his arm.

Tim nodded and headed for the front door. Shortly later, the bell rang, and in a few minutes, the dining room was filled with hungry ranch hands.

The day passed uneventfully as men went about their daily chores, and Strykes helped where he could. Boone was never far away, his eyes constantly scanning the land for any sign of movement. They both knew that Lucas wouldn't take much longer to make his move. Strykes wanted this fight over with. He was tired of hiding and afraid for LaRisa. If Lucas ever got his hands on her, death would be a blessing.

Late in the evening, his mood hadn't improved as he stood at the loft door looking out. He wondered if the best thing would be to leave and go after Lucas alone. There was no reason for anyone else to get hurt in this fight. He knew Boone would want a hand in it, but Strykes didn't want to risk the chance of the man getting killed. He would be a father soon, and Strykes wouldn't be responsible for getting him killed.

"Bret," LaRisa called from below.

What the hell was she doing here at this hour? "LaRisa, you should be inside," he told her and continued to scan the moonlit ranch.

"I brought you a few more blankets. I thought you might get cold."

Strykes descended the ladder and saw her standing there in the pale light with folded blankets in her arms. He took them from her and muttered his thanks. He held on to them to keep from pulling her into his arms. If he did, he wouldn't let her go.

She stepped closer to him. "Do you think they'll come tonight?"

"No," he said, shaking his head. "Lucas is too smart for that. He knows what kind of men he's up against here. He'll wait until I'm alone someplace before he does anything."

"Then that means you can't go anywhere," she said. "You have to stay here."

The hope in her eyes made his heart sink. "LaRisa." He tossed the blankets on the fresh pile of hay in the corner. "Me being here puts you all in danger. I think it would be better if I took off on my own."

Fear twisted in her heart. "You can't go. Lucas will kill—"

"I have to go." He reached out and cupped her cheek. "I'm putting all of you at risk by staying here. Sooner or later, he's going to try and use one of you to get to me. I know how he thinks."

"But you're safe here," she told him, trying to think of a way to make him stay.

"I'm trapped here. There's a big difference."

"But—"

"LaRisa." He placed a finger on her mouth to silence her. "I can't stay. I know what Lucas will do to you if he ever got his hands on you. I won't risk that happening. I have to leave and draw him away from you."

Tears sprang to her eyes, and she didn't bother trying to blink them back. She didn't want him to go. She loved him. The thought of him leaving was unbearable, but the thought of him getting shot and dying was even more horrible. He was right, though. He was trapped here. But he was protected and could be kept alive.

His eyes grew soft. "Please don't cry."

It was only then that she realized the tears had found their way to freedom and were flowing down her cheeks. "I don't want you to go." Her voice was tight.

"I won't be gone forever." He brushed her tears away with his thumbs. "I'll come back."

"You better." She grabbed the back of his head and forced his mouth to hers.

Strykes stood unmoving, trying to decide whether to push her away or take her in his arms. He knew the right thing would be to make her stop and send her back to the house, but a part of him refused to do so. When she made a noise of frustration and traced her tongue across his bottom lip, the only thing he could do was take her in his arms and kiss her back. She let out a sigh, and her body melted against his.

A desperate need to feel his strong, warm body washed over her, and she quickly fumbled with the buttons of his shirt. When the last button was free, she splayed her hands over his chest, drawing a ragged groan from him. He let her push his shirt off over his shoulders until it fell to the ground. Then she let her hands roam over his chest, back, and arms.

In record time, Strykes managed to get her bodice off and flung it aside. His big hands cupped her breasts, and he ran his thumbs across her nipples. She moaned and arched her back to him, offering all she could.

In no time at all, he had removed the rest of her clothes. Taking a step back, he admired her pale naked body in the moonlight. He would never tire of looking at her. He muttered a curse before he grabbed a blanket and spread it over the hay. Then he reached for her and nearly threw her on the blanket. He covered her body with his and kissed her deeply as his hands moved over her.

LaRisa let out a moan as his lips traveled down her neck and a shiver ran through her when he traced the delicate line of her collarbone with his tongue. Her body was on fire, and her mind could focus on nothing but Strykes.

Then lightning shot through her as he claimed one of her taut nipples and pulled it into his mouth. Her fingers laced through his hair, and she held him to her breast. She felt his hand slide down her stomach, and she eagerly opened for him as he cupped her womanhood.

A cry of pleasure escaped her before she could think to stifle it. His mouth claimed hers again as his fingers worked their magic on her. Soon her hips were rocking with the rhythm of his hand.

"Please" was all she could say. "Bret, please."

With the sound of passion surrounding his name, he moved away from her and quickly removed the rest of his clothes. In no time at all, he was with her again, his naked flesh touching hers. He lay over her and claimed her mouth again. She moaned and shifted against him in a way that caused him to shudder.

He pushed her beneath him, and in one powerful thrust, buried himself to the hilt. She let out a cry, her fingers digging into his back. He held himself ridged as he savored the feel of her. He planned on leaving to find Lucas, and he wanted to relish every moment with her first.

She let out an uneven moan and buried her face in his neck. Her breath was hot and her mouth wet as she kissed and nibbled at him. He braced himself on both hands and looked down at her. Her green eyes were glazed with passion.

"Please, Bret." She shifted her hips beneath him.

With a groan, he claimed her lips once more and ground himself against her. She let out a cry and clung to him. He moved within her, his hips thrusting slowly and gently, trying to keep control as he brought them both pleasure. She eagerly moved against him, matching his rhythm. Gradually the rhythm picked up, harder and faster. Their bodies moved together until they were both covered in a fine sheen of sweat and their moans and gasps blended.

With no warning, the pressure that had built up inside her exploded with enough power to take her breath away. A blinding storm of pleasure crashed over her as her body spasmed with release. She knew Strykes had found the same release when he groaned between clenched teeth and his body went rigid. She felt him pour his seed into her, and her body eagerly took all he had to give. When he was spent, he collapsed onto her.

It seemed like an eternity passed until their breaths slowed and their hearts were no longer racing. Strykes rolled off her and pulled a blanket over them. He settled back, and she nestled herself against him. He pulled her closer and placed a kiss on her damp forehead.

"When it's over, I'll come back for you," he promised, hoping it wasn't a mistake.

Chapter Eighteen

From somewhere through the sleepy haze of his mind, Strykes heard the metallic click of a gun being cocked. His body immediately rolled to one side, and he grasped the butt of his pistol just as a boot came down and pinned the gun to the ground. Looking up, he stared into the barrel of a rifle. His eyes moved up the barrel and saw a set of dark-blue eyes, blazing with rage. Those eyes belonged to Matthew Reeves, and he was mad as hell.

"Get up, get your clothes on, and get off my place before I kill you."

Strykes glared back at Matthew. He wanted to argue, but the rifle pointed at his forehead made him hold his tongue. From beside him, he felt LaRisa stir. She blinked around with sleepy eyes.

"Pa?" she said, and then her eyes focused on her father standing there with a gun aimed at Strykes's forehead. "Pa!" She sat up quickly, reaching for the blanket to cover her nakedness.

"Matthew!" Shyfawn's voice came from behind her husband.

She stood there holding a tray of coffee and biscuits. When her eyes saw LaRisa and Strykes sitting in the hay covered only in blankets, she set the tray aside. "What's going on?" she demanded as she came forward.

"Isn't it obvious?" Matthew growled.

Shyfawn stared from her husband to her daughter and Strykes. "Yes, it is."

"You son of a bitch. I'll kill you for this," Matthew growled with rage.

"Pa, please don't shoot him," LaRisa begged her father.

"Didn't you hear anything I said yesterday?" he demanded, but he didn't wait for his daughter to answer. "I warned you against him!"

"I love him!"

Both Matthew and Strykes gaped at her. "You what?" they asked in unison.

She stared wide eyed at Strykes as her blurted confession stunned her. "I-I love you."

Strykes felt as if a giant fist clenched his gut. "LaRisa," he whispered and took her in his arms, the rifle pointing at him forgotten.

"Matthew." Shyfawn put a hand on her husband's arm. "Come on. We'll sort this out later."

He lowered the rifle slightly and looked at his wife. "Shyfawn, he just…" He couldn't find the right words as he growled them out. "With our daughter."

"Give them a minute," she said softly.

Reluctantly, Matthew lowered the rifle and turned to his wife. "I'll kill him later."

Shyfawn took Matthew by the arm and led him from the barn. "Remember, you…" She smiled at him. "With me before we were married," she pointed out.

"That's different," he snarled.

Shyfawn chuckled and cast a look back at her daughter. Strykes held LaRisa close and kissed her softly. Shyfawn smiled, and they left the barn, leaving the two lovers.

***

Strykes had forgone lunch at the house, not wanting to face Matthew Reeves yet. He knew the confrontation was coming, and he wasn't looking forward to it. Can't fault a father for wanting to protect his daughter.

Strykes had taken up his post at the loft door, looking out over the land for any sign of movement. Nothing so far. It was late in the afternoon when Strykes received the not-so-anticipated visit from LaRisa's father.

"Strykes, get down here," Matthew growled from below.

With a groan of dread, Strykes descended the ladder to find the man standing near the open barn doors. He was angry but no longer looked like he wanted to murder him. But Strykes would not rule out that possibility just yet.

"Matt, I know you're angry, but—"

"You're damn right I'm angry! And damn it, you're going to marry her."

"I'm what?" Strykes blinked at him.

"After what happened, I think it's the best thing to be done." He glared at Strykes. "Or I could string you up for what you did."

"Now isn't the best time for me to be getting married to anyone," he told Matthew.

"Oh, now is the perfect time," Matthew informed him. "What if she's pregnant?"

Strykes staggered back as if Matthew had hit him. "Pregnant?"

"Yeah. It does happen, you know?"

"I know it happens, but—"

"All it takes is once," Matthew informed him.

Strykes was about to point out that he and LaRisa had been making love for quite some time, but he didn't think that bit of information would help him at the moment. It would probably get his head blown off.

Strykes dragged a hand over his face and took a calming breath. "I can't marry her."

Matthew glared at him. "I don't see where you have much choice."

"Matt, I'm not a good man," Strykes told him flatly. He fought to find the right words. "I love her, but if I stay with her, I could end up hurting her."

"If you leave her, it'll rip her heart out," Matthew informed him. "I can't say I approve of this, but Shyfawn is right. For the first time in many years, LaRisa is happy. Much to my disappointment, it's because of you. You can't leave her."

Strykes swore and jammed his hand through his hair. If he stayed, he could very well kill her himself. He wanted to be with her, but she wouldn't be safe. He had many of his father's traits, and he was scared as hell of being too much like the man.

"This isn't a good idea," Strykes said roughly.

Matthew glared at him. "You should have thought of that before you bedded her."

Truth was, he had thought about it, but his need for her won out. His need for her could very well be the thing that would kill her. "Matt, I can't marry her," he said regretfully and met the man's angry eyes. "I could kill her."

Matthew's eyes hardened. "What the hell do you mean by that?"

Strykes let out a long breath. He didn't want to tell Matthew, but the man needed to know the truth. "My father was a mean bastard. I-I'm a lot like him. I'm afraid that one day I will be him, and I'll hurt LaRisa."

Matthew's eyes softened slightly as he thought over Strykes's words. "As much as I don't like it, I've seen you with her, and I don't think you'd ever hurt her." He looked at Strykes for a moment. "And as you pointed out earlier, if you tried to hurt her, she could easily kill you."

Strykes nodded. "She could. But I may not give her the chance." He felt his stomach roll as images of his father went through his mind. "If I'm like my father, she won't have a chance to get her hands on me," he said with distaste.

"What'd your pa do?" he ventured.

"Things no man should do to his family." He met Matthew's eyes evenly. "I'll marry her, but if I ever raise a hand to her, I want you to kill me."

Matthew didn't have to think about his answer. "You can count on that."

***

"Strykes?" Boone said as he entered the barn in the light of predawn. "What're you doing?"

Strykes glared at Boone as he tossed the saddle onto the bay horse. "I'm going to find Lucas," he said simply as he pulled the cinch tight. "I have to put an end to this."

Boone said nothing as he went to where his blue roan was stabled. He took down the bridle hanging on the stall gate and slid it onto the horse before he led the animal from the stall. He moved to the saddle rack and pulled down his saddle and blanket to toss on the roan's back.

"What the hell are you doing?" Strykes demanded as he watched Boone saddle the horse.

Boone met Strykes's glare evenly. "I'm not letting you take on Lucas alone. I'm coming with you."

Strykes wanted to argue but held his tongue. He guessed that if anyone should go with him, it should be Boone. The man had run with Lucas long enough to know what the man was like. He knew how Lucas thought, and Strykes also knew he couldn't keep Boone from coming with him.

"Fine," Strykes grumbled. "But don't get in the way."

Boone smiled at him as he pulled the cinch tight. "I'm just coming along to make sure you don't get killed."

Strykes swore under his breath as he led his horse from the barn. The bullet slammed into the side of the barn near his face. He swore loudly as splinters bit into his cheek, and he dove for the relative cover of the wagon. More bullets kicked up dirt around him and thunked into the side of the wagon. From around the ranch, there was return fire from the men on the ranch as they emerged from buildings to take up the fight.

"Strykes, you dead?" Boone asked from just inside the barn door.

"No, damn it," he growled.

The gunfire from the trees where the ambushers were hidden, faded away as they retreated. Strykes looked around for his horse. The animal had bolted and was now up behind the house. Strykes scrambled to his feet and ran for the corral. He grabbed a halter and lead from the fencepost as he threw open the gate. Strykes caught a black mare and swung up onto her bare back. He turned her in the direction Lucas and his men had gone. He heard Boone yell something as the mare took off at a gallop. Luckily, she was a runner, and he would catch up to Lucas in no time. He only hoped he wouldn't catch a bullet along the way.

The rain pelted his face and soaked him to the bone. Strykes hoped the mare wouldn't slip and fall in the mud as he rode hell-bent after Lucas. He couldn't let the man get away. He had to end this once and for all.

Strykes followed the tracks left by Lucas and his men as the rain beat down on him. He couldn't let them get too far ahead of him, or the rain would wash the tracks away. He wondered how far behind him Boone was. He wouldn't be able to take on Lucas and the men with him by himself.

A gunshot split the air, and Strykes felt the bullet skim across his upper arm. He turned the horse toward the small amount of cover the trees near the river provided, hoping it wasn't a mistake. He knew some of Lucas's men would be hidden there as well. The mare lost her footing at the sudden change of direction and went down in the mud.

Strykes jumped clear as the mare fell, and he hit the ground hard, rolling to a stop in the mud. Gunshots echoed, and he scrambled for the cover of a downed tree. He crouched behind the big cottonwood's trunk. Bullets dug into the bark, and he could hear Lucas shouting over the noise. After a moment, all was quiet.

"Strykes," Lucas hollered through the driving rain. "Get out here and face me."

Strykes pulled his pistol and began cleaning the mud from it with his wet shirt. "So your men can shoot me when I stand up?" he laughed. "Not a chance, Lucas."

"You still don't trust me?" The humor in his voice drifted to Strykes. "That hurts my feelings."

"You don't have feelings," Strykes grumbled at his pistol as he did his best to clean the mud from it. "Send your men out unarmed," Strykes called to Lucas. "They can leave, and you and I can kill each other in a fair fight."

Lucas was quiet for a long moment, as if contemplating Strykes's request. "You got a deal," he yelled over the storm. "Drop your guns and get out of here," he ordered his men.

Strykes knew Lucas was lying. At least one man would stay behind and make sure that Lucas didn't die. Lucas couldn't beat Strykes in a fair gunfight, and they both knew it.

"Son of a bitch!" someone yelled, and gunfire quickly followed.

Strykes chanced a look over the tree trunk, being sure to stay behind a thick branch for some cover. Through the driving rain, he could see Lucas and his men scattering for cover as Boone and several men rode in. Lucas's men took cover and fired back as the men on the horses fired and took cover as well.

Strykes saw Lucas break away from the firefight and run like the coward he was. Without thinking, Strykes leaped to his feet and took chase. Lucas was heading to the thicker cottonwoods near the river. The flooding river gave Lucas little chance of escape.

Lucas ran flat out along the riverbank, with Strykes closing the distance rapidly. He had a clear shot at Lucas's back, but Strykes wasn't a back shooter. He wanted to see the life leave the man's eyes as he faced him down and killed him.

Lucas cast a glance over his shoulder to see Strykes gaining on him. Sliding to a stop in the mud, Lucas aimed his pistol at Strykes. He pulled the trigger, and Strykes felt the bullet slide across his side. He swore and closed the distance to Lucas quickly. Lucas fired again, and the hammer fell on an empty chamber.

The man turned to run, but Strykes took him to the ground hard. Both men lost hold of their pistols as they fell into the mud. They traded powerful blows as each man tried to get the upper hand. Lucas landed a solid blow on Strykes's temple, and he toppled over. Lucas got to his knees, and his hands closed around Strykes's throat. His blue eyes held rage and satisfaction, as he knew he would finally get his revenge.

Strykes pushed at Lucas, but the man had a fierce grip on his throat. He squeezed hard, cutting off Strykes's air and threatening to crush his windpipe. Strykes brought his fist around to punch Lucas in the face. He heard the satisfying crunch of the man's nose as it broke. Lucas howled in pain, and his hold loosened. Strykes hit him again, and Lucas toppled back.

"You bastard," he growled as he held his bleeding nose with both hands.

Strykes gasped for breath as he got to his feet to face the man. "I'm going to kill you, Lucas," he said, his voice rough. His throat felt raw.

Lucas shook his head. "I've waited too long to get even with you. I'm not about to let you kill me."

"You should have gotten out when I did," Strykes told him as he tried to get air into his lungs.

"You shouldn't have killed Fisher," Lucas growled, anger and pain in his eyes.

Strykes glared at him. "My mistake was not killing you that night too. I won't make that same mistake now."

Strykes moved to face off with Lucas. The man's eyes darted around the muddy ground in search of a pistol. They were lying behind Strykes, and he couldn't get to them without going past the big man. He opted for the knife in his boot, pulling it in one swift motion. He held it easily in his hand and faced off with Strykes.

"Come on," Lucas taunted. "Try to kill me."

Strykes glared at him for a moment before he moved in. Lucas was good with a knife, but Strykes refused to back down. Lucas might kill him with the knife, but Strykes was going to take the man to hell with him.

Lucas made a slice at Strykes's stomach when he was in striking distance. He easily avoided the move as they circled each other. Lucas gave him a cold smile and lunged for Strykes. Sidestepping, Strykes struck out with a fist to connect with the side of Lucas's head.

"You're not going to win this one," Strykes told him coldly.

Lucas laughed and moved in to slash at him again. Strykes's hand snapped out to grip Lucas by the wrist. He squeezed and twisted the man's arm until he let go of the knife. Strykes released his arm and landed blow after blow to the man's face and stomach. Strykes threw a punch at Lucas's head, and he ducked. He missed, and it threw him off balance as he slipped in the mud for a second.

Lucas took advantage and shoved his shoulder into Strykes and pushed him along, heading him to the riverbank. Strykes did his best to get his footing in the slippery mud as Lucas pushed him toward the flooded river. There were a lot of things Strykes could do, but swimming wasn't one of them. The river was flooding, and Strykes knew he didn't stand a chance if Lucas pushed him in.

Near the riverbank, Strykes let his knees buckle, and he went down. He used Lucas's momentum and catapulted the man over the top of him. Lucas swore until he went over the bank and down into the river. His scream of fear was cut short as the water closed in over his head and he was pulled under.

Strykes got to his feet, his eyes searching the churning water for Lucas. He saw the man come up twice, then he was pulled under again to be swept down the river. Strykes wiped the blood and rain from his face as he continued to look for any sign of Lucas. After a few moments of seeing nothing, Strykes turned to retrieve the pistols and Lucas's knife.

At the sound of horses pounding toward him, Strykes felt his stomach tighten. The pistols would be useless, caked with mud like they were. He only had a knife, and that was no match for men with guns. He turned to see the riders emerging from the trees and sagged with relief when he recognized Travis's gray horse and Boone's roan.

Strykes stood there, trying to catch his breath and assess the damage to his arm and side where the bullets had grazed him. He might need a few stitches, but he was far from mortally wounded. He looked up and watched Travis and

Boone ride toward him, their clothes soaking wet and rain dripping off the brims of their hats.

"Where is he?" Travis asked as he pulled his horse to a stop and dismounted.

Strykes jerked his head toward the river. "In there."

Travis lifted a brow at him. "Really?"

"I didn't intend to throw him in, but it happened," Strykes told him flatly.

Travis nodded and looked at the raging river. "Hell of a way to get out of hanging." He looked at Boone. "Gather up a few of the men and ride down the river until you find his body."

"Will do," Boone told Travis, then looked at Strykes.

Strykes saw the doubt in the man's blue eyes. They shared a look Travis couldn't see. Both men knew Lucas. He was like a cat with nine lives. They wouldn't count him dead until they both saw his body strung up by the neck or full of bullet holes. Preferably both. Then struck by lightning just to be safe.

Boone held his eyes as he walked his horse past, and Strykes nodded in understanding. Lucas wanted Strykes dead, and he would kill Boone as well. They would have to watch their backs and stay close to their women. Lucas would stop at nothing now. If he was alive, he would make damn sure they suffered before they could kill him.

"Did you get the rest of them?" Strykes asked Travis.

Travis shook his head. "Two got away, and with the rain, their tracks will be gone before we can catch them."

Strykes looked past Travis to see several riderless horses that had belonged to the outlaws grazing in the trees. "Let me catch one of those horses, and we'll help Boone find Lucas. I won't rest easy until I see that man dead."

Chapter Nineteen

LaRisa paced the length of the porch again, her eyes scanning the prairie and road for any sign of Strykes. When she had seen him ride out after the men trying to kill him, her heart had nearly stopped. He had ridden out in the driving rain after a man who wanted him dead. She had heard the echoing of the gunfire from down by the river, and when all went silent, she could not fight her tears. LaRisa had been so afraid something had happened to him. The rain had stopped long ago, and they still hadn't returned.

"He'll be back," Shyfawn said as she stepped out onto the porch.

LaRisa stopped pacing to look at her mother. "How can you be so sure?"

Shyfawn gave her a soft smile. "Because all we can do is hope for the best. I worry every time your father leaves on a cattle drive or when he helps Travis. But I know he'll do all he can to come home to me, and he always does."

LaRisa nodded, though she didn't share her mother's confident spirit. Would Strykes come back to her? She loved him, but did he love her? She was sure he did. He had to. He had become such a part of her life in the short time he had been in her cabin with her. Now that she knew what love was, she didn't think she could live without it. Without him.

"Any sign of them?" Matthew asked from the bottom of the porch steps.

LaRisa looked at her father and shook her head. She had been so focused on the road that she hadn't noticed her father walk to them from the barn. He and several men had stayed behind to guard the ranch in case Lucas doubled back. Thankfully, all had been peaceful after the outlaws fled.

"Strykes will be back," Matthew told her, seeing the fear in his daughter's eyes.

"LaRisa, let's go get dinner started," Shyfawn said softly. "They'll be hungry when they return."

LaRisa cast another look down the road and reluctantly nodded before following her mother into the house. She remained silent as she helped her mother prepare the evening meal. Shyfawn had always cooked for the men working for them. Even when she had a house full of children and Matthew wanted to hire a cook for the ranch hands, Shyfawn had refused.

Outside, the dogs barked, and LaRisa stilled to listen. She heard Travis call a greeting, and she bolted for the front door. She paused outside, and in the fading light of day, she saw the men riding in. Her eyes instantly found Strykes, and her heart surged with love for him as the fear and worry left her in a rush.

Tears burned her eyes as she hurried down the steps and ran through the ranch yard. Strykes swung off his horse and gathered her in his strong arms to hold her tightly to him. He held her in a bone-crushing grip for a long time. She could hardly breathe, but she didn't care. He was alive, and he was safe. He drew back and kissed her deeply, and she eagerly kissed him back. They broke apart when several of the men hooted and gave catcalls.

"No wonder he was in a hurry to get back," Boone jeered as he dismounted.

Strykes shot him a glare as he slid his arm around LaRisa to pull her close to his side. "You just don't worry about it," he snapped, even as he fought a smile.

"Did you get him?" Matthew asked as he approached, his expression disapproving as he looked at his daughter and Strykes.

LaRisa looked up at Strykes to see him exchange a glance with Boone. "What is it?" she asked, feeling her stomach tighten with dread.

"Nothing," he told her simply. "We got him. Two of his men got away, but they won't hang around."

"Lucas went into the river," Boone explained. "We didn't find him. But we'll go out and retrieve what's left of his body tomorrow. He's probably washed to Nebraska by now, though."

Again, LaRisa noticed the look Strykes and Boone shared. She wanted to ask what it meant, but she knew they wouldn't tell her. Strykes was alive and with her again. Nothing else mattered.

"I'll take care of your horses," Matthew told the men. "Go in and get something to eat."

Strykes didn't argue as LaRisa took his hand and led him to the house. The rest of the men followed, and Shyfawn had a table full of hot food for them in no time. The men ate hungrily and savored the hot coffee as it eased the chill of rain from their bodies.

LaRisa wanted to sob with relief that Strykes was alive and well but controlled herself. Was this what it was going to be like loving a former outlaw? How many times would his past come looking for him? Now that Lucas was gone, would it be safe for them to be together? She sighed and tried not to think about it. She would take things a day at a time.

***

Strykes left the marshal's office and stepped out into the sunny day. Travis had wanted him to come to town to make an official statement of what had transpired the day before. Travis also informed him that when Lucas's body was found, Strykes had a considerable reward coming his way.

He stepped off the boardwalk and headed down the street to the café. Inside, his eyes found the table LaRisa and her family sat at. He wasn't sure why Matthew had insisted that they all ride into town together, but he wasn't going to argue. He was already on the man's bad side, and he didn't want to make it worse.

"Finished already?" LaRisa gave him a small smile as he sat beside her. "I thought it would take longer."

"Nope. Short and sweet," he said simply.

They ate the meal in mostly silence, but Strykes didn't mind. Though Matthew and Tim cast him hostile looks, he enjoyed the moment of eating a meal with a family. It had been more years than he cared to think about since he had last had a family meal. Even then, it was rarely pleasant.

When they finished, the family made their way outside.

"Get in the wagon," Matthew ordered.

"Are we going home already?" LaRisa asked. "Don't you want to get a few supplies while we are in town?"

"No," he said flatly. "We're going to the church so the two of you can get married."

LaRisa stared at her father for a moment as if he had lost his mind. "Married?" She looked at Strykes to see his expression carefully controlled.

"Yes. The way the two of you have been carrying on, I think it's the best thing to do," Matthew informed her. "Get in the wagon."

LaRisa looked for any kind of reaction from Strykes, but he betrayed no emotion. Her heart hammered in her chest. She had never thought she would ever get married, let alone her father forcing her to marry. She swallowed hard. But if she had anyone in the world to pick to marry, it would be Strykes. He had awakened feelings in her she had never known, and now she desperately needed those feelings. He had treated her like a human, and he had never been afraid of her. She also knew that she was desperately in love with him.

***

The marriage ceremony was quick and small, consisting of her parents, brother, and the elderly preacher, James. Afterward, they went back to her parents' house for a meal before heading to her cabin. Their cabin.

The ride to the cabin was made in mostly silence. She tried to engage Strykes in conversation, but he only grunted or remained silent. So she settled for watching Saber dart through the fields looking for whatever it was dogs found interesting. She wished Strykes would talk to her and tell her how he felt about the whole situation. He had been very reluctant to say I do, and it had made her heart ache. His mind was occupied and far away, and his expression was cold.

They reached her cabin and rode to the barn. Strykes helped her strip her saddle from her horse before he turned them out into the corral. Without a word, he turned and walked to the cabin. LaRisa followed him with tears in her eyes. He opened the door and put his hand out to stop her when she tried to walk in. She blinked several times before she met his eyes.

Strykes looked at her for a long time. Her eyes were shiny with tears, and he felt his stomach tighten. He had been too occupied with his own thoughts of the past and the uncertainty of his future to notice she was upset. He reached out and gently touched her cheek. Strykes took a deep breath to calm his racing nerves. He could do this; he could be her husband, and if he ever thought he might hurt her, he would leave. Swallowing hard, he felt his chest grow tight. He knew he could never leave her. Not for any reason.

LaRisa let out a startled squawk when he suddenly scooped her up in his arms and carried her into the cabin. Strykes kicked the door shut before Saber could dart in and carried her to the bedroom. He set her on her feet next to the bed and took her face in his big hands. He bent his head and kissed her tenderly. When he lifted his head to look at her, she had tears swimming in her eyes. He gave her a soft smile and felt her body relax.

"LaRisa Strykes," he whispered. "I like the sound of that."

She smiled at him. "So do I."

Strykes took his time undressing her, touching and kissing every part of her as he revealed her soft skin. When they were both shed of their clothes, he laid her down on the bed and covered her body with his. She kissed him urgently, but he was in no hurry.

"Bret, hurry," she begged as she wrapped her legs around him.

Strykes smiled at her. "You've been my wife for half a day, and you're already bossing me around."

"Yes, I am. Now hurry," she ordered, though humor laced her voice.

Strykes had no intention of hurrying. LaRisa was his now. All his. Forever. He swallowed hard as he looked down at her, and the old fear hit him once again.

Her brow puckered, and she reached up to stroke his jaw. "What is it?"

Instead of answering, his mouth found hers for a deep, stirring kiss. He would push his fear back and enjoy whatever time he had with her.

When he entered her body, he felt the peace she gave him, and every worry he felt vanished. He made slow, sweet love to her for the rest of the day. When they were both spent, they fell asleep wrapped in each other's arms.

***

LaRisa pitched hay from the hayloft to the waiting animals below. She was a married woman now. Never in all her life did she ever think it would happen to her. She had always imagined she would be the crazy witch everyone was afraid of. She would live away from people and collect cats or some nonsense like that. How life had changed for her.

She screamed as powerful arms wrapped around her and pulled her back. The pitchfork clattered to the floor as she was lifted and thrown down into the hay. A heavy body landed on top of her.

"Strykes, what the hell?" she snapped, instantly knowing it was him.

Humor danced in his eyes, and he gave her a slight smile. "I came to see what you were up to," he told her as he nuzzled her neck.

She laughed and wrapped her arms around him. "My chores. Nothing fantastic."

"Maybe not," he said as he unbuttoned her bodice. "But I'm sure this will be much more enjoyable."

"You think so, do you?" she said a bit breathlessly as his hand covered her bare breast.

"Yes," he said with a groan. He loved that she didn't wear underthings. "I do think so."

She arched against his palm as he dragged his thumb over her nipple. He grabbed her and rolled onto his back, pulling her across him. His hands ran down her body and over her hips to pull at her legs until she straddled him. He worked her dress up her legs until he touched her bare thighs.

"Strykes, what are you doing?" she asked again.

"Enjoying my wife," he said against her skin.

"Here?" she gasped. "Now?"

"Yes, and yes," he said as his hand moved over her nest of curls to cup her.

She moaned and pressed against him. "But it's the middle of the day."

He chuckled. "Yes, it is." He nipped along her collarbone. "And I can see everything."

She felt herself flush and a surge of heat went through her. She didn't object when he pulled off her bodice and tossed it aside.

"Hello, the house!" a voice rang out from outside.

"Shit," Strykes grumbled. "Great timing."

Strykes wanted to choke Boone for interrupting them. He helped LaRisa to her feet before he descended the ladder into the barn. He straitened his clothes and brushed hay from his hair before he stepped outside.

"Afternoon, Boone. Come to pay a social call?"

"Not really." His expression was serious. "I came to talk about Lucas."

"Did you find him?" Strykes asked, though he knew the answer.

Boone dismounted and shook his head. "No body."

Strykes felt his gut twist. "Damn."

"Strykes, nobody could have survived that river," Boone told him.

"But you have your doubts."

Boone let out a long breath. "We found scraps of his shirt, a boot, and gun belt scattered for miles down along the river. He couldn't have survived. If he didn't drown right off, the current would have beat the hell out of him on the rocks. I don't like the idea of having no body to spit on, but he has to be dead."

Strykes swore in frustration. "You don't believe that any more than I do."

Boone nodded. "Travis and I are going to go back out and look again. The body could be in Nebraska by now, but we're going to go see what we can find."

"Find him," Strykes said with a growl. "I won't rest easy until I know he's dead."

"You and me both."

Chapter Twenty

Strykes and LaRisa rode into town to the curious looks of the townspeople. He knew that every citizen within a hundred miles knew the witch had married a former outlaw. A wry smile tugged his mouth. They made quite the pair.

They dismounted before the livery, and Strykes took the reins of her horse. "I'll look after him."

"I won't be long." She reached into her saddlebags for her bag of herbs for Doc Sam.

"Take your time and go visit Leslie. I'll help Roper for a while and gather my few possessions to take home."

She smiled and gave him a quick kiss before she hurried away.

Strykes watched her for a moment before he turned and went into the livery. Home. It was a strange feeling to him to finally have a home after so many years of drifting or being on the run. He had never imagined his life would turn out this way.

He entered the livery to see Quinn disappear into the tack room and Jonny harnessing two horses. Like him, they had a questionable past but had found a new beginning in Rimrock. And like him, they were never without their well-worn pistols.

"About time you came to town to get a little work done," Quinn teased as he came from the tack room.

Jonny only grunted at him as he led the two harnessed horses out through the back door. He was a man of few words, but he was a dangerous man with that Sharps rifle of his.

He chuckled. "I have a wife to provide for now."

Quinn stepped forward and offered Strykes his hand. "Congratulations. Being married is pretty great. I know I'd be lost without Kelly. I'll take care of your horses."

Strykes handed him the reins and left the livery. The town was busy. His eyes went to the depot. People came and went. Supplies were unloaded into the waiting wagons. Supplies. He looked at the mercantile. They needed a few things for LaRisa's cabin.

Crossing the street, Strykes stepped up onto the boardwalk to find Logan McCord and Rafe Reeves seated in the shade, eating penny candy.

Logan gave him a wide grin. "Greetings, cousin."

Strykes groaned and prepared himself for a ribbing from LaRisa's cousin. "I forgot I'd be getting you in this deal."

Logan laughed, his gray eyes dancing with humor. "Me and half the town. You're part of a big family now."

Strykes couldn't help but feel pleased. He liked the idea of being part of a big family.

Apparently, her family accepted him. Other than her father and brother.

"Would you look at that?" Rafe said as he pushed his hat back on his head and stared down the street at the woman coming out of the boardinghouse.

Strykes turned and looked at her as well. She was indeed beautiful. She wore a fine dark purple gown with a black sash that made her waist look even smaller. Her hair, a deep brown, was piled up, and ringlets hung down around her shoulders. She stood talking to Leslie, and she appeared to be giving the young woman directions.

"Wonder what brought a woman like that to town," Rafe remarked, once again taking in the way she was dressed.

"I don't know," Logan said, his eyes fixed on her.

"Logan."

"Huh," he said absently.

"You're droolin'," Rafe said with a laugh.

Strykes chuckled as Logan quickly looked away from the woman to glare at them, but his gray eyes soon found their way back to her. She and Leslie were just standing there talking like women tend to do. Then Leslie turned and gestured across the street at the three men lounging under the overhang. The young woman turned quickly and looked at them.

"Bret!" the young woman hollered, and lifting her skirts, she made her way down the steps into the street.

Strykes stiffened, and his heart stuttered as he narrowed his eyes at the woman. Not very many women in this world called him Bret. One was at Sam's, three were in New Orleans as far as he knew, and one was dead.

He took a step forward as the young woman approached. She trotted toward him, a slight limp in her step. Recognition hit him hard in the stomach, and he didn't know whether to shout with joy or faint dead away from shock. He muttered something like a curse and started toward her. What in the hell was she doing here?

"Hey, Strykes, what is it?" Rafe called after him.

He ignored Rafe and continued across the street to the woman. She smiled with delight, and he couldn't help but smile back at her. She held her dress out of the dirt and ran toward him, her limp more pronounced. When she was close enough, she threw herself into his arms, and he held her against him tightly, lifting her off the ground as he swung her around. She laughed with joy until he put her back on her feet. She hugged him tightly. He had to stoop over to keep a hold of her and keep her feet on the ground. Damn, he had forgotten how short she was and how small her body was.

"I wasn't sure I'd ever see you again," she sobbed with happiness against his chest.

He pulled back and looked down into her flawless face, her cheeks wet with tears and her pale-green eyes shining with happiness. Not trusting himself to speak, he pulled her back into his arms and hugged her again. This time, her feet lifted from the ground. She laughed and clung to him.

"Strykes, you'd better get out of the street before someone runs you over," Rafe called.

Strykes pulled back and took the woman by the hand and led her back to the boardinghouse. He had no desire to face Rafe and Logan at the moment. He didn't want them asking a bunch of nosy questions. Not to mention the fact that he didn't want to talk to anyone until he found out the reason this woman was in Rimrock.

They entered the boardinghouse, and Strykes pulled her into the parlor. "What're you doing here?" Strykes demanded as they sat on the sofa.

A frown came over her beautiful face. "Aren't you happy to see me?"

Strykes sighed and took her hands in his. "Of course. I'm glad to see you. I'm just surprised, that's all."

She smiled again. "I knew you would be. Oh, you have no idea how long it took me to find you. I was starting to think something bad had happened to you."

Strykes wanted to ask her to define *bad*, because he had his fair share of bad. Instead, he reached out and fingered one of her dark ringlets. He shook his head in wonder.

"You sure grew up to be a beautiful woman. How old are you now?" He felt slightly embarrassed that he couldn't remember.

She seemed not to care. "I'm nineteen now. I figured I was grown up enough to come looking for you."

Leslie came in then with a tray of tea and cookies. She placed it down none too gently on the table before them and stood with her hands on her hips. Being heavily pregnant diminished any effect of intimidation she might have wanted to project.

Strykes didn't miss the anger in her dark eyes. "Yes?"

"Aren't you going to introduce me to your *friend*?"

He didn't miss the way she said the word, and a smile tugged at his lips. "Leslie Cain, this is Willow." Her eyes narrowed on the girl, and he tried not to laugh. "My baby sister."

The change in Leslie was immediate. She smiled broadly, and there was nothing but friendliness on her face. "Oh, my. It's good to meet you. Why in the world didn't you say something earlier?" Leslie's face flushed with embarrassment. "I was thinking the worst about you. Here I thought you were being untrue to LaRisa right in front of the whole town."

Willow looked at him. "Who's LaRisa?"

"LaRisa." Strykes started. "Well, you see she's..." He looked up at Leslie.

"Oh." She nodded and put a hand on her belly. "I think I better get off my feet for a few minutes. It was good to meet you." And she disappeared from the room.

"Bret, tell me," Willow said, her large pale-green eyes studying him.

Strykes cleared his throat. "LaRisa is my wife."

"Your wife!" Willow leaped to her feet. "Why didn't you tell me?"

Strykes stood and rammed his fingers through his hair. "Well, it just happened, and I haven't had time to write."

"Where is she? I'd like to meet her," she said as she tried to move around him to the door.

Strykes stepped in front of her. "There will be time for that. But first I want to know where Skye and Ashton are."

"We split up to look for you."

"Why didn't you stay together?" Strykes snapped and headed for the door, Willow on his heels. "This isn't New Orleans. Who knows what kind of lowlife they've run into."

Outside, he quickly walked down the street. Willow had to jog to keep up with him. His eyes scanned the people around the depot. No Skye or Ashton. Would he even recognize them? It had been such a long time since he had last seen them.

"There she is," Willow said as she pointed down the street.

He turned to see Skye standing in front of the mercantile, talking to Rafe. Strykes groaned and ran a hand over his face as he watched Rafe with Skye. He was going to have to kill every young man in town to keep them away from his sisters.

"Come on." He took Willow's hand and moved toward Skye.

Rafe gestured behind Skye, and she turned. When she saw Strykes, she let out a cry as she ran the distance to him. Strykes thought her cry sounded more anguished than happy. He saw the tears on her cheeks as she threw herself into his arms. She wasn't nearly as short as Willow, but he wrapped his arms around her and lifted her from the ground, holding her tightly against him. She sobbed and clung to him as her body trembled.

"Skye, honey," he whispered, his throat tight. Jesus, he had missed her. He missed all his sisters.

He set her back on her feet, but she continued to cling to him. Willow stepped forward and brushed her hand over Skye's black hair. Strykes looked at her and saw the tears in those pale-green eyes. He let go of Skye with one arm and wrapped it around Willow to pull her close. He stood in the street holding his sisters, and he didn't give a damn who saw.

"Bret," Skye choked out as she set into another fit of sobbing.

Willow reached out and stroked a hand over Skye's head. Strykes looked at Willow and saw the worry there. Something was wrong. He scooped Skye up in his arms and carried her to the boardinghouse. Willow followed, wiping at her eyes.

Strykes went into the parlor and sat down, cradling Skye against his chest. Willow sat beside him and reached out to take Skye's hand.

"Skye, it's all right," Strykes soothed, and he looked at Willow for an answer.

Willow swallowed hard and blinked back tears. "It's been a very long trip," she said with a smile. "We're just tired and overly emotional."

He gave her a skeptical look. "What else?"

Willow tilted her head and gave him a sister look. "Bret, we haven't seen you in nearly seven years. We have missed you dreadfully, and now we finally get to be with you. You make it sound like there's something wrong with that."

He studied her for a moment as he held a trembling and sobbing Skye. "These aren't tears of happiness," he told Willow flatly, and Skye buried her face against his chest.

She lowered her lashes for a moment before she looked at him and smiled brightly. "You've been away from us for far too long." She gave him a reassuring pat on the arm. "Don't you think that seeing you after seven years is a little overwhelming for us?"

"Willow, I—"

"We didn't know where you were or if you were even alive until a few months ago," Willow said as tears filled her eyes. "We were so afraid you had been killed in the war." She blinked and tears fell, but she gave him a sweet smile. "You should have seen us when we got your letter. We all cried for hours."

"Where's Ashton?" he asked and saw her smile falter for a split second, and Skye nestled closer to him.

"She's still in New Orleans," Willow told him. "She had some things to take care of." She gave him that "everything is fine; stop acting like a big brother" look. "We hope she'll come soon." She gave him another bright smile and wiped her cheeks. "Aunt Francy sends her love."

Strykes said nothing as he looked at Willow. Ever the actress. She could stand on the coals of hell with a bright smile and make anyone believe she was in paradise. He understood that emotion could overtake them at seeing him after so long, but there was more to it. He was going to find out, even if he had to choke it out of Willow.

"Bret." Skye's voice was soft. "I don't mean to make such a fuss." She pulled back and looked at him. "Please don't worry over us," she told him as she wiped her eyes. "I just got emotional." She said the last around a sob.

Strykes looked into Skye's clear, almost colorless blue eyes, eyes just like his. Eyes like their father's. He felt his stomach tighten, and he studied her. Eyes that once had sparkled now were flat and dead. The dark circles beneath them emphasized the haunted soul she carried inside. What had happened to his family in the many years of his absence? He suddenly felt like a bastard for leaving them for so long. He shot Willow a hard look that demanded an explanation.

Willow smiled and let out an excited gasp. "Tell Skye about LaRisa."

He gave her a scowl, and she only batted her long lashes at him. She was the smallest person he knew, and the fact that he couldn't intimidate her irritated him. Ever since they were children, she had gone toe to toe with him, never backing down. Even though he towered over her and could break her in half, it didn't faze her at all. He gave her a small smile. He loved the hell out of her.

"LaRisa"—he turned to Skye's haunted eyes—"is my wife."

A flicker of happiness flashed in her eyes, and she smiled at him. "You got married?" The happiness was fleeting, and shadows crept into those pale eyes once again.

"He did," Willow said happily. "Tell us about her."

Strykes let out a long breath. He would go along with Willow's change of subject. He would find out the truth later. Right now, he wanted to enjoy being with his sisters. He told Skye and Willow about LaRisa.

When they asked about the years after the war, it was his turn to paint a prettier picture than the reality of it. He didn't want them to know what he had done or about the men he had killed. He would tell them later.

They would all come clean with each other later.

Chapter Twenty-One

It was late when Strykes left the boardinghouse. Leslie had insisted that his sisters stay with her and in no time had them each tucked into a room. He frowned as he walked to the livery to fetch their horses. LaRisa hadn't come to see Leslie. Had she been at Doc Sam's the entire time?

Strykes entered the livery and found the stall his horse was in. He didn't see LaRisa's black horse anywhere. He slipped the bridle onto his horse and led her from the stall.

Quinn descended the loft ladder. "I was wondering if you were ever going to come back."

"Where did LaRisa go?"

Quinn shrugged. "Home, I guess. I asked her if she was going to wait for you, but she said that you had your hands full."

Strykes let out a groan. She had probably seen him hugging Willow right there in the middle of the street, big as life. "Thanks."

Strykes quickly saddled his horse and headed for home. Again, the thought of having a home pleased him. And now that his sisters were with him, he wasn't sure life could get any better. He frowned as he rode. When would Ashton join them?

Strykes urged his horse into a faster pace, and it was nearly dark when he reached the cabin. He cared for his horse before turning her out into the corral with the black horse. He jogged to the cabin, eager to see LaRisa.

Strykes opened the door and ducked as a plate came whistling through the air at his head. It crashed against the wall and clattered to the floor in many pieces. His eyes flew across the room to find LaRisa grabbing up another plate. He closed the door and moved toward her.

"You son of a bitch!" she bellowed as she let the next plate fly.

Strykes ducked, and it smashed into the wall. "LaRisa, what the hell is wrong with you?" he demanded as he marched toward her.

"Go to hell!" she snapped and reached for another plate.

Strykes grabbed her wrist and whirled her to face him. "Stop that. We're going to have to get more plates if you keep that up."

"I don't care." Hot, furious tears burned in her eyes. "How could you?"

"What are you talking…" His voice trailed off. "Oh, that."

"Yes, that!" she snapped. "Hanging all over some woman right there where everyone can see you."

He tried not to smile. She was jealous. "LaRisa, it's not—"

"If you don't like me, you could have at least said so and not go sneaking around." Tears spilled down her cheeks.

"LaRisa." He wrapped his arms around her and pulled her to him. "I do like you, and I'm not sneaking around." She opened her mouth to argue, and he continued quickly. "That was Willow. My baby sister."

She blinked at him. "Your sister." She was speechless for a moment. With a groan, she dropped her head to rest on his chest. "I'm such an ass."

He chuckled and held her to him. "I wouldn't go that far. You're just a jealous wife."

"I'm so sorry I threw the plates at you." She was clearly embarrassed at her behavior.

He kissed the top of her head. "It will remind me to never make you angry." He put a hand under her chin and made her look at him. "You are the only woman in the world I want to be with. There will never be anyone else."

"I'm sorry I mistrusted you."

He kissed the tears from her cheeks. "You didn't know she was my sister." He smiled at her. "Hell, if I saw you in the street hugging on some man, I'd probably shoot him."

"I guess we should be glad I didn't shoot her," she said with a slight smile. "When will I get to meet her?"

"Tomorrow. You'll meet Willow and Skye tomorrow," he said and took her face in his hands. "Right now, I have plans for you."

She smiled through her tears. "Really?"

"Yes," he whispered and lowered his mouth to hers.

She made no objection, but he knew she wouldn't when he pulled her into his arms and kissed her deeply.

***

Strykes stood in the doorway in Leslie's parlor and watched his sisters and LaRisa talk. Willow did most of the talking, but she had always been like that. He smiled slightly. Willow had always been so full of life. He looked at Skye. She said very little. That wasn't like her. What had happened to her in his absence?

LaRisa laughed, drawing his attention back to her. She seemed at ease around his sisters, though he had noticed she wore her gloves today. Her fear of hurting someone was back. She hadn't worn gloves in so long; he had almost forgotten about her fears. Images of her taking Martin's energy filled his mind. He had died quickly from her touch.

His own fears suddenly plagued his mind again. He looked down at his own hands. Large, scarred hands. He used these hands to do legitimate work, making things to help people. For so many years, he had only used them to destroy and kill. Kill with a gun, knife, or his bare hands.

These hands killed their first man when he was twenty and hadn't stopped until two years ago, when he was given a second chance. But knowing what his hands were capable of scared him. Knowing what he could become scared the hell out of him.

Strykes looked at his sisters. They knew what could happen. They had seen their father's brutality firsthand. Willow had been subjected to it. Their father had beaten her and broken her leg to keep her from getting away. She would forever have a limp to remember that day. The day he had killed their father.

Footsteps behind him caused him to turn. Leslie was walking toward him from the kitchen.

"Are you and LaRisa staying for lunch?" she asked as she looked into the parlor.

"Yes," Willow said with a smile.

Strykes chuckled. "I guess we are."

LaRisa stood. "I'll help you, Leslie."

Strykes stepped away from the door to let LaRisa pass. She gave him a warm smile before she and Leslie disappeared into the kitchen. He entered the parlor to sit on the sofa with Willow.

Willow looked at him for a moment. "Bret, what's bothering you?"

Strykes almost laughed. Willow could always see right through him. "I'm scared, baby sister."

Her pale-green eyes filled with worry. "Scared? You're never scared."

"I am now," he told her honestly. "Being with LaRisa scares the hell out of me."

Willow took his big hand in her small one. "Bret, you love her, and she makes you happy."

He nodded. "Yeah, I've never felt like this before. The first time I saw her, I felt something inside me come to life. I tried to fight it, but I couldn't. I love her so much, and it scares me."

She smiled. "It's time for you to be happy and to have a good life."

He met his sister's eyes evenly. "What if I'm like him, Willow?"

She gave him a stern look. "You are nothing like him. You spent all of our childhood protecting us from him." Tears shimmered in her eyes. "You did what you had to do."

He swallowed hard. "But I couldn't save our mother."

She reached out and caressed his cheek. "You were a child. You did all you could to save Mama, and he almost killed you for it."

"Bret." Skye's voice choked with emotion. "Our father may have killed our mother, but you saved the rest of us from him."

Strykes looked at Skye. Her pale, haunted eyes filled with tears, and her cheeks were wet. He held his arm open for her, and she left her chair to sit beside him. He held each sister close and was so grateful to have them in his life again.

"You're not like him," Skye whispered. "You'll never be like him."

"Don't be afraid to love her," Willow told him.

Strykes swallowed hard and pulled his sisters close. He felt his eyes burn, and his throat grew tight. He loved LaRisa, and he was afraid. The thought of ever hurting her or any children they might have tore at him. It was a fear he carried with him every day.

***

Strykes walked down the boardwalk to the marshal's office. The past week with his sisters in town had been wonderful, but his mind was on their safety. Knowing that Lucas could still be out there worried him. If the man found out about them, he wouldn't think twice about using them to get to him. He could keep LaRisa safe, and knowing that Boone was in the boarding house with his sisters eased his mind somewhat.

He entered the marshal's office to see Travis seated at his desk looking through the latest wanted posters. Once again, Strykes was thankful that he wasn't on one of them.

Travis looked up. "Good morning. Come to confess any evildoing?"

Strykes chuckled. "You know I'll never tell."

Travis stood. "Well, I can always try. What can I do for you?"

"Any news about Lucas?"

He let out a long breath and shook his head. "He's dead, Strykes. There is no way he could have survived the river. The reward money will be coming to you."

Strykes wanted to believe him, but deep down, he knew Lucas was out there somewhere. "I have to be sure my family is safe from him, and I won't relax until I'm standing over his dead body."

Travis nodded in understanding. "Maybe, but odds are good that he's already dead. But I'll send out a few wires to the towns downriver to see if anyone has found a body."

"Thanks, Travis."

Strykes left the marshal's office, not feeling any better than when he arrived. At least Travis was willing to look into it a little deeper. Anything would be better than not knowing. If no body had been reported, then he would know Lucas was still alive.

"Bret," Willow called out.

He turned to see her hurrying after him. "Good morning, little sister."

When she reached him, she grabbed his hand. "Come with me. I have something to show you."

Strykes had no choice but to go with her, as she kept a hold of his hand and dragged him with her. She led him down a side street to a two-story house with a large covered porch.

"Here it is," she said happily.

He shrugged. "It's a house."

Willow smiled at him. "We have purchased this fine house."

He blinked at her. "You what?"

She laughed. "Bret, don't sound so shocked. Come in and see."

Strykes followed her into the empty, dusty house. "You're staying in Rimrock?"

She nodded. "Won't it be great? All of us together again."

"Minus Ashton," he said quietly.

Her smile faltered for only a second before she turned and went through the house. "Come see the big room in the back," she said with an excited hop.

Strykes grumbled and followed her. It pleased him they would be staying, though he found the reasons behind the sudden appearance and decision to stay questionable.

She stopped in the middle of the room and twirled. He couldn't help but laugh at her.

"This will be the sewing room," she told him happily. "We are going to have a wonderful dress shop."

Strykes nodded. "That is a great idea. This town could sure use a couple of fine seamstresses." He smiled. "You could make me a shirt that actually fits."

She smiled brightly. "You'll be the best-dressed man in town." She looked around the room. "It's perfect."

"Willow." His voice was soft. "Why are you *really* here?"

She laughed. "Dresses."

"No. Why did you come to Rimrock?"

She scoffed. "Because you're here. We came to see you. It just so happens we like it well enough to stay."

He tamped down his frustration. "The truth, Willow. You sent no word of a visit. You showed up out of the blue and with only the clothes on your backs. What's going on?"

She laughed and waved a hand in dismissal as she gave him a sweet smile. "Bret, you—"

"Don't!" he snapped, and her smile faded. "Don't put on an act for me, Willow. I know you too well. What the hell is going on? I want a straight answer."

Strykes actually took a step back at the immediate change that came over her beautiful face. The smile disappeared, and the happy mischief in her pale-green eyes vanished, leaving them cold and flat. Fear, anguish, and helplessness shadowed her flawless face. Her slight frame nearly crumpled, and he could see her body tremble.

"Willow." His voice was soft. "Tell me what happened. What happened to Skye? Where is Ashton?"

She swallowed hard and looked at him with hollow eyes. "We had a problem with a wealthy gentleman in New Orleans." She looked away from him for a long time.

He took a step toward her, wanting to comfort her. "Willow?"

"No!" Her head came up, and she looked squarely at him. "Let me finish before you touch me."

He held his ground as she tried desperately to hold on to her emotions. He felt his stomach tighten, and his heart pounded. What she was about to tell him wasn't going to be good. He knew she would crumble if he touched her now. He would comfort her after she had told her story.

She took a breath. "He was an artist, and we hired him to paint a picture of the three of us to give to you. It was a beautiful painting of us. You would have liked it," she told him and hesitantly continued. "Things went bad one day." Tears filled her eyes. "I'm not going to tell you what happened." Then anger filled her eyes. "But he won't be bothering us ever again."

Strykes felt sick. His gut twisted, and anger slammed into him. He could guess what had happened when he thought of Skye's haunted look, and he wanted to smash something. Clenching his hands into tight fists, he tried like hell to keep the anger under control. He could be a violent man, and now was not the time to let his rage take over.

"We took his money and ran," Willow continued quietly. "Ashton put us on the train and said she'd catch up. She wanted to make sure nobody followed us." The tears in Willow's eyes spilled free. "I'm so scared something bad happened to her," she said as she choked on a sob.

Strykes closed the distance to her and gathered her close. He held her small body tight as she cried. Her arms wrapped around his waist and clung to him desperately as she let the sobs take her over. He wrapped an arm around her shoulders and held her head to his chest with his free hand. Her small frame shook as she cried out all the emotions that she had been so carefully hiding.

Strykes held her until her sobs became hiccups. "I never should have left you girls."

She shook her head against his chest. "You had to go, Bret. Those Jayhawkers would have killed you."

He swore silently. She was right. He would be dead if he had stayed. The war had closed in and swallowed him up. After the war, he had gotten tangled up with a group of outlaws instead of going to New Orleans like he should have.

Jesus, if he had been there, he could have protected them.

Strykes let out a long breath. "I'm sorry, Willow. I should have been there for you girls."

She drew back and looked up at him. "You've always been there for us. You kept us safe for so long, but you can't protect us forever," she told him as new tears fell.

He took her face in his hands. His precious baby sister always saw life so clearly and was ready to take on any challenge. She was a small woman, but she never let that hold her back.

"Ashton, Skye, and I have had a good life the last several years," she told him honestly. "Considering our childhood, we thought Aunt Francy was an angel sent to save us." She smiled at him in reassurance. "We never had it so good."

"I'm glad," he said, brushing her tears away. "I knew you'd be safe with her. But I should have come to be with you after the war. I could have been there for you."

"Bret, we've had hard times all our lives," she informed him. "Each of us has been hurt in a different way. But we had each other, and we made it through." Tears filled her eyes again. "We'll get through this too."

He slowly nodded and held her to him again. How could such a small person be so strong? She had grown up into an amazing woman. She was right. They always survived the hard times. As long as they had one another, they could make it through anything.

Chapter Twenty-Two

"Come on, get moving," Quinn ordered good-naturedly. "Finish getting this grain unloaded, and you can go home to your wife."

Strykes chuckled. "How long will it be before you stop teasing me about being married?"

"Probably a couple years."

"Looking forward to it," he muttered.

Strykes tossed the sack of grain over his shoulder and headed down the row of stalls. A gray horse snorted at him as he walked past. He stopped dead in his tracks and backed up a few paces. He narrowed his eyes on the gray, and his heart lurched. The big, ugly hammerhead horse looked back at him. Strykes stepped to one side until he could see the animal's hip. He nearly dropped the grain sack. A 3 broken bar 7 brand was stamped there for all to see. The other horse Lucas had stolen.

"Are you going to stand there or unload grain?" Quinn's voice was filled with humor as he walked past with a bag of grain.

"Where'd you get this horse?" Strykes asked, not taking his eyes from the gray.

"Bought him from a fella this morning." Quinn frowned. "Why do you ask?"

Strykes turned to him. "What did he look like?"

Quinn shrugged. "Blond hair, blue eyes, looked to be about twenty-five or so. He was pretty beat up, though. Had recent scars across his face and arms."

"Shit," Strykes muttered. Lucas had survived the river like he had suspected. "Are you sure?"

"Yeah."

"Did he say where he was going?"

Quinn shook his head. "No. Last time I saw him, he was headed for the saloon."

Strykes swore under his breath as he finished unloading the grain. At least he now knew that Lucas was alive. How Lucas had survived the fall he didn't know, but he had, and he would want revenge. Want it mighty bad. He wouldn't stop until he had put Strykes in the ground, and he would stop at nothing to do just that.

If things were only that simple, but they were more complicated now. He was a married man, and his sisters were in town. Lucas had several targets to pick from. How in the hell could he keep them all safe?

He knew how. He had to leave, had to find Lucas before it was too late for the ones he loved.

***

Strykes sat at the table and poked at the food on his plate. His mind went over and over how to handle the situation with Lucas, and the solution was always the same. He would have to go after the bastard.

"Is everything all right?" LaRisa asked hesitantly.

He nodded and tried to give her a smile. "Fine."

"A-are you sorry you married me?"

Strykes blinked at her. "What?"

She let out a helpless sigh and looked across the table at him. "You don't seem very happy today. You act like I've got the plague when you're around me."

"Oh, no, LaRisa." He reached out and took her hand in his. "I'm sorry; it's not you. It's just…"

Just what? How could he tell her that Lucas was still alive and would come to kill him? He had a feeling it was only a matter of time before the man came and hurt her or one of his sisters. He wanted to tell her. He didn't want to keep secrets from her, but he also didn't want her to worry about him. She wouldn't let him leave town without a fight. She would demand that he stay and fight it out here. He couldn't take the chance. Tracking Lucas down and meeting him on his own terms was what he had to do. It was the only way to keep the ones he loved safe.

"You don't like being married, do you?" she said softly.

"LaRisa, it's not—"

"I know it will work. You just have to give it time. You'll like it. Just wait and see."

He raised her hand to his lips and kissed her fingers. "I never said I didn't like it."

A shiver ran through her as his lips caressed her fingers and hand. "You're not sorry you married me?"

He came around the table and knelt before her. "I'll never be sorry for marrying you." How could he tell her she might be sorry she had married him? How could he tell her he could turn into a bastard and hurt her? He couldn't. There was so much he couldn't tell her.

He reached out and cupped her cheek in his large hand. "I love you, LaRisa."

Tears sprang to her eyes, and she could barely speak. "You do?"

He smiled slightly. "Yeah, I do."

She caught a hint of sorrow in his tone, and his eyes held a touch of sad regret. But before she could think on it further or ask him, he kissed her tenderly. She wasn't about to argue with him. Throwing her arms around his neck, she kissed him back.

With their half-eaten meal forgotten, Strykes picked up LaRisa and carried her to the bed. In no time at all, he had shed both of them of their clothes and laid her down. Stretching out beside her, he eagerly took a nipple into his mouth. She arched against him and offered him all she could. Reaching down, she took his hard shaft in her hand, drawing a groan from him, and he gently bit down on her nipple, bringing a cry from her.

He found her mouth again and poised himself above her. Her hands went to his waist, urging him down. He took her in one swift motion. He thrust into her over and over again, and she met each one. Soon her world shattered, and she clung to him as he poured his seed into her.

"Tell me again."

Strykes gave her a slow smile. "I love you."

With a contented sigh, she pulled his head down and kissed him once again. She shifted her hips, and he let out a groan. "Make love to me again," she whispered against his lips.

"No. I have a better idea." He grabbed her around the waist and rolled onto his back. "You make love to me."

She wasn't about to object to that. She eagerly made slow, sweet love to him. And then later he returned the favor. At some point, she looked up to see Saber on the table, finishing their meal. She would scold him later. Much, much later.

***

Strykes silently slid out of bed and dressed. Saber whimpered and looked up at him. He reached down and scratched the animal behind the ears, assuring him that all was well. Even though it wasn't.

He sighed and glanced at LaRisa as she slept. Her rich auburn hair fanned around her and fell across her bare shoulders. God, she looked like an angel. How could he leave her? It would be the hardest thing he would ever have to do, but it wasn't safe for her if he stayed. He knew he couldn't tell her he was leaving. She wouldn't let him go.

When things quieted down and he got this business with Lucas settled once and for all, he would come back for her. His throat tightened. If she would still have him. He knew the best thing he could do was kill Lucas and keep riding, but he couldn't. He loved her, and though the possibility of hurting her haunted him, he couldn't leave her. Leaning over, he lightly kissed her on the lips. She sighed and murmured his name. He swallowed hard and turned from her.

He strapped on his gun belt before picking up his saddlebags and rifle. Quietly, he opened the door and cast one last look at her. If he made it through this alive, he'd come back and do his damnedest to be a good husband to her. With heavy saddlebags thrown over his shoulder and an even heavier heart in his chest, he closed the door and left the woman he loved lying peacefully in bed.

***

The morning sun drifted in through the window, warming the cabin. LaRisa stretched and yawned. She smiled and rolled over to put an arm around Strykes. There was only empty space to greet her. She lifted her head to see he was not there. Her gaze darted around the room. He was nowhere to be seen.

"Bret?" She got out of bed, wrapping a blanket around her naked body.

She frowned and looked down at Saber. He wagged his tail happily and bounded to the door. She opened the door for him, and he ran out to do his business. Her eyes strayed to the outhouse, and she closed the door. That was probably where he was. There was nothing to worry about.

She smiled and went about making coffee for him when he returned. She would wake him up, and then she had plans for him. Would she ever be able to get enough of him? She certainly hoped not. Turning from the stove, she grabbed a couple of pieces of wood to get a fire going, then stopped. Her eyes drifted back to the bed. His pistol was gone from the bedpost, as were his rifle over the fire, his hat, and his saddlebags.

The wood clattered to the floor, and she rushed to the door and flung it open. A quick look at the corral told her that his horse was gone. Her heart dropped to her stomach, and her legs gave out on her. She slid to the doorstep and sat there, staring blankly at the corral. He had gone, left her without so much as a goodbye.

LaRisa could only sit there and stare out over the land. Her chest hurt, and she felt the tears on her cheeks. Saber trotted to her and sat beside her. He gave a whine and nuzzled his head under her arm. She choked on a sob, threw her arms around him, and cried. Her heart was shattered, and she knew she would never heal.

***

Strykes tried to push LaRisa from his mind as he rode, but he couldn't. He felt like a son of a bitch for leaving her, but he had to do it. His family wouldn't be safe until Lucas was dead. He couldn't lose LaRisa or his sisters to that bastard, and he knew Lucas would go after them.

Strykes was lost in his thoughts when his horse's head came up, and his attention riveted on the trees in front of them. His hand went to his pistol as he made out the shape of a horse and rider in the shadows. He swore under his breath. It was a blue roan and a man he knew well. He rode up to the man and stopped to glare at him.

"You're slipping, Strykes. I could have killed you," Boone told him hollowly. "Good thing I happened along to hold your hand."

Strykes pinned him with a hard look. "What the hell are you doing here?"

Boone pulled back his coat to show the badge to Strykes. "Travis thought I'd better tag along to make sure you kill Lucas all legal."

"How the hell did Travis know I was going after Lucas?" he snapped.

"I told him you would." Boone moved his horse in beside Strykes. " I know you would have refused any help we offered."

"Damn it, Boone," he bit out. "I don't need you on this."

Boone grinned. "See? There you go refusing help." He urged his horse forward down the trail. "You didn't really think I'd let you go after Lucas alone," he said, knowing full well Strykes would follow him.

Strykes rode up beside him and fixed him with a hard look. "Boone, I'll shoot that horse out from under you if you don't go back."

Boone met his hard look with one of his own. "Strykes, you may still scare the hell out of me, but I rode with that gang too. You're going to need me whether you like it or not. Travis deputized me to make sure you don't do something stupid, and I want to see Lucas just as dead as you do. I'm coming with you."

Strykes tamped down his anger and glared ahead of him. Boone was right. He would need help, and there wasn't another man around that Strykes would rather have with him. The two of them had never seen eye to eye when they rode with Fisher and Lucas, and they had never been friends.

Boone had ridden out of the gang, and that hadn't set well with Fisher. They had trailed him to Rimrock, and when it was all over, Strykes had ended up helping Leslie escape Fisher. He had killed the man to save Boone and Leslie. Lucas had slipped away, but Strykes had never dreamed the man would come after him. Lucas had come for him, and now Strykes had to kill him to keep the ones he loved safe.

Since their arrival in Rimrock, Boone and Strykes had come to a truce and had respect for each other. Hell, they were close to being friends, though neither one would admit it.

"It's going to take me a little time to find Lucas," Strykes pointed out.

"No, it won't. He's going to find you. Hank is at the saloon letting it be known that you have left town. We both know that Lucas will have spies in the saloon and around town. Hank, Logan, and Rafe will tell anyone who asks that you headed north out of town."

"You got those three in on this too?"

"Hank asked to be a part of this," Boone said flatly. "He knows Lucas was the one who shot him, and he wants a piece of the action."

"That I understand, but why would Logan and Rafe take a hand in this?"

Boone grinned at him. "I think they want to impress your sisters."

Strykes groaned as he dragged a hand over his face in frustration. "I'm going to have to kill them, I just know I am."

Boone laughed. "Worry about that later. Right now, we have an ambush to plan."

Strykes grumbled a curse, but he knew Boone was right. He would worry about his sisters' possible suitors later. He would kill Lucas and keep those he loved safe. Then he would do whatever he had to do to keep his sisters safe from their admirers.

Chapter Twenty-Three

Tears blinded LaRisa as she rode her black horse toward her parents' house. Saber trotted happily ahead of her, eager to play with his friend and oblivious to her misery.

As Buster barked and ran to meet them, LaRisa saw her brother step from the barn. Tim wasn't the one she wanted to see right now; she wanted her mother. But as she pulled her horse to a stop, Tim's expression held worry as he reached up to help her dismount. LaRisa fell into his arms, sobbing.

"LaRisa, what happened?" he asked as he brushed his hand over her back to comfort her.

LaRisa could easily feel the awkwardness her brother felt. He hadn't hugged her or comforted her since she was a child. He had always been her rock and her confidant. It had broken his heart when she had pulled away from her family and chose to live on her own.

"What's wrong?" he asked again.

"St-Strykes is gone," she choked out as she clung to him.

"Gone?"

"I-I woke up and-and he was gone."

"That son of a bitch," he growled angrily.

All LaRisa could do was sob. She was barely aware that he had steered her toward the house until they reached the porch steps. Tim helped her into the house and into the parlor.

"Ma!" he called as he seated LaRisa on the sofa.

Hurried footsteps sounded on the stairs, and her mother appeared in the parlor wearing her nightdress. Matthew quickly followed, dressed for the day ahead.

"What happened?" Shyfawn asked as she rushed to her daughter. She sat on the sofa and held LaRisa close.

Tim answered for her. "Strykes left her."

"Oh, honey," Shyfawn soothed.

"That bastard!" Matthew spat angrily. "You should have let me kill him."

"Matthew!" Shyfawn snapped. "Not now."

"I'll tend to Blackie," Tim said as he left the house.

"He-he left, Mama," LaRisa sobbed. "Yesterday, I woke up, and he was gone. I-I thought he'd come back, but..." She couldn't finish.

"That no-good son of a bitch," Matthew growled.

LaRisa didn't have to look to know her mother was giving him a stern look. She couldn't blame her father for being angry. He had known what kind of man Strykes was, and now he had been proven right. He had warned her against Strykes, and she had ignored him. Instead, she had gone out to the barn that night, and the next morning her father caught them together.

"I'm sorry, Daddy." She lifted her head and met her father's angry eyes. "I should have listened to you."

Matthew let out a long breath and moved to sit on the sofa beside her. "If you had, you still would have been hurt. You loved him then."

LaRisa did her best to control her emotions. "Maybe, but it would have been easier. Things are more complicated now."

For a moment, her father waited for her to continue, then a dawning realization washed over his face. "You're pregnant."

She nodded, and Matthew stood suddenly. LaRisa watched him pace to the window, his hands clenching and unclenching at his sides. Her eyes went to her mother, and she saw nothing but compassion in their emerald depths. LaRisa's throat threatened to close off again.

"I'm sorry, Mama. I feel so ashamed." She buried her face in her hands.

"You don't have anything to be sorry about," Shyfawn told her as she pushed LaRisa's hands aside and took her face in her hands, forcing LaRisa to look at her. "And having a baby is nothing to be ashamed about."

She couldn't keep her voice from shaking. "Mama, I may be married, but he's not here. He left me."

"Does he know about the baby?"

"No, I hadn't told him yet." She looked down at her gloved hands. "Maybe if I had, he wouldn't have gone."

Shyfawn sighed. "Honey, these things happen. Strykes wasn't the type to settle down. I'm surprised he stayed in Rimrock as long as he did."

"But we were married. He should at least have taken that into consideration. I would have gone with him."

Shyfawn shook her head. "It would have been no kind of life for you. Just think, if you had to pack that little one all over the country."

"Now he'll just grow up without a father. What am I going to tell him when he asks about his father?"

"Tell him he was hit by a train," Shyfawn said casually.

"Mama! I can't tell him that."

"You're right," she said with a slight smile. "You don't have to worry about that for a few more years. I'm sure we'll have come up with a good story by then."

"I don't want a story. I want Bret," she said, fresh tears running down her cheeks. "I can't do this on my own."

"You won't have to," Matthew said as he turned from the window and came toward them. "Your mother and I are here for you."

LaRisa stood and threw her arms around her father and sobbed into his shoulder. Matthew wrapped his arms around her and held her close as she cried. When she had no more tears, she pulled back and wiped at her cheeks.

"You look exhausted," Shyfawn told her as she stood. "Go upstairs and rest. I'll bring breakfast up to you."

LaRisa nodded and headed for the stairs. She wasn't tired, but she didn't want to cry any longer, and she wanted to be alone. Shyfawn followed her up the stairs into her bedroom.

"Thanks, Mama." LaRisa tried to put on a brave smile, but she knew her mother saw right through it.

Shyfawn took LaRisa into her arms and hugged her tightly. "You'll get through this, honey."

Her tears overflowed as she hugged her mother back. "But it's so hard."

"I know, but your father and I are here for you." She pulled back and wiped LaRisa's tears away. "We love you, and nothing could ever change that."

She swallowed hard and nodded. "Mama, I-I'm scared."

"There's nothing to be afraid of," she assured her. "Now, you get some rest," Shyfawn told her and kissed her on the cheek before she left and shut the door.

With a heavy sigh, LaRisa crossed the room and sat down on her bed. She knew her parents would be talking about her and her condition. No doubt her father was ready to hunt Strykes down and kill him, but she knew her mother wouldn't allow that. Her mother knew she loved Strykes and that would never change, even if he were dead. She had thought that he loved her too, but she had been wrong.

Had Strykes only wanted to use her body? She had given herself to him, and now her life would never be the same. He had changed her body, her heart, her soul, and her future in just a few months. How could she have been so stupid? No man in his right mind would want her. He had used her and cast her aside. That was a hurt she could never get over.

Tears streamed down her cheeks as she let her hands drift to her stomach. She was afraid. Afraid for her baby. What kind of mother was she going to be? Could she even hold her baby? She looked at her gloved hands and let her sobs take her.

***

Strykes rode down the dusty road at a casual pace. He knew he was exposed and an easy target, but he had to let Lucas see him. His shoulder blades itched as if feeling the barrel of a rifle taking aim at him.

"Great idea you had, Boone," he grumbled as he rode.

Strykes knew Boone's plan would not work until they lured Lucas to them. The only way to do that was to use Strykes as bait. Yesterday, they had laid out a trail for the man to follow, and Strykes hoped it hadn't been too obvious.

The only way to beat Lucas at the game was to play it his way. Ambush. Boone, Rafe, Logan, and Hank were in position, waiting for the action. He hoped they knew what they were getting into. This was going to get violent and bloody.

Without moving his head, Strykes let his eyes scan the surrounding area. He had spied a rider following him not long ago and knew that Lucas would hit anytime. Strykes only hoped he would be on the right part of the trail when it happened. If Lucas hit too soon, Strykes was a dead man. Dying was something he intended to avoid. He had a wife to get home to.

Before his thoughts could stray to LaRisa, Strykes pulled his thoughts back to the present. He couldn't let himself get distracted. He was doing this for her, and he would get it finished once and for all.

The crack of a rifle split the air, and Strykes immediately kicked the mare into a gallop as he felt a bullet whiz by his head. He stayed on the trail until he saw the riders giving chase. Seven of them, and Lucas was one. This would end today.

Strykes turned the mare off the trail and headed her through the trees. He wouldn't be an easy target now, and that sent a wave of relief through him. He kept the mare at a pace guaranteed to let the pursuers gradually close the distance between them.

Finding the deer path Logan had told him to look for, Strykes turned the mare down it. Good. With any luck, the plan would go off without a hitch. Being unfamiliar with the area, Strykes had to go by what Logan had told him. When the low-hanging tree branch came into view, Strykes knew he had followed the directions correctly.

"Got one shot at this," he grumbled as he kicked his feet from the stirrups.

As the mare galloped under the tree, Strykes reached up and grabbed the branch. The mare kept on down the trail, and he dangled from the limb. Oddly, Strykes compared it to being lynched, hanging from a tree branch as the horse bolted away. He had managed to avoid such a thing so far and was disturbed by his thoughts.

There was no time to ponder such things. The galloping horses were getting closer. He had to hide. Strykes walked his hands down the branch until he was at the tree trunk and swung his body before letting go, to be sure he landed on the thick bed of pine needles to leave no tracks. He quickly spotted the cluster of rocks and dove behind it.

He listened to the horses pass by, following the path his riderless horse had gone. Strykes chanced a peek around the rocks and smiled as two riderless horses galloped past. Rafe and Logan had done their job, picking off the men in the rear without anyone noticing. Strykes himself hadn't seen them hiding. They were good.

The outlaws would soon realize his horse had no rider. He had to get moving. He ran back to the trail to see Logan and Rafe mounted, leading a horse for him behind as they came toward him.

"How the hell did you hide the horses?" he asked as he mounted the horse.

Logan grinned. "They were lying down and covered with brush."

There was no time for more questions as they fanned out. Strykes rode down the trail after the outlaws while Logan and Rafe rode on either side of him, gradually moving farther out, leaving the outlaws no room for escape if they turned back.

Shouts ahead of him implied the outlaws had found his horse without a rider. As well as discovered, they were missing two men. Strykes urged his mount faster. They had stopped too soon. Boone and Hank were waiting farther down the trail. Their plan had just gone to hell.

Strykes emerged from the trees to see the outlaws stopped and looking around uneasily. One spotted him and drew his pistol. Strykes wasted no time in pulling his own. The man's shot went wide, but Strykes hit him in the heart. Two men wheeled their mounts and galloped away.

"You damn cowards!" Lucas yelled after them. "Get back here!"

The remaining man with Lucas pulled his rifle from its scabbard. He had barely put it to his shoulder when Strykes fired, hitting the man low on his side. His second bullet took him in the chest, knocking him from his horse.

Lucas met his eyes as his horse barreled down on the man. He drew and fired at Strykes, his shot going wild. Strykes fired; his bullet clipped Lucas's ear. Lucas whirled his horse around as Strykes fired again, causing him to miss. The man was going to run, but Strykes would not let him get away.

Holstering his pistol, Strykes moved his horse in after Lucas. He caught Lucas before the man's horse could build up speed. Launching himself from the saddle, he hit Lucas, and the two men went to the ground hard. They rolled and came up on their feet to face each other.

"You're not going to get away from me this time," Strykes growled.

Lucas put a hand to his ear. His hand came back bloody. "You going to shoot an unarmed man?" he taunted. "That's not your style."

Without taking his eyes from Lucas, Strykes walked to where the man had dropped his pistol and picked it up. "I'll let you have this back, and you can face me in a fair fight."

Lucas snorted. "That was why you made a lousy outlaw. You had to make sure every fight was fair. I don't know why Brown didn't kill you."

"Because he needed my gun." Strykes stopped a few paces from Lucas and tossed the man's pistol at his feet. "Pick it up."

Lucas rolled his shoulder, as if to ease a muscle sore from the fall. "It's too bad, you know. I'm about to make that pretty wife of yours a widow already." He gave a shrug, then fixed Strykes with a malicious smirk.

"Remember once I told you I'd send you to hell before me?" Strykes asked, his voice hard and cold. "I intend to make good on that. Pick it up."

Lucas slowly bent over to retrieve his gun. He straightened and grinned. "You only have one bullet left."

"I only need one."

His grin faltered, and fear flickered in his blue eyes. His hand, still holding the gun, came up. He didn't have time to pull the trigger before Strykes drew and shot him in the forehead. His body flew back, and he landed sprawled on the ground.

Strykes reloaded his pistol as he walked to Lucas. His eyes were open and staring unseeing at the blue sky above. Holstering his pistol, Strykes stood there and looked down at the lifeless man. His family was safe now.

Horses coming toward him caused him to draw his pistol and turn. He saw Boone riding toward him and relaxed. He returned his pistol and waited for him to close the distance between them.

"Glad you're not dead," Boone said as he dismounted.

Boone stood over Lucas's body and looked at him for a moment before he turned his gaze to Strykes. They looked at each other for a long time, and Strykes weighed his options. It might have been a fair fight, but he had still killed three men. Boone could arrest him for that. Lucas might have been a wanted man, but Strykes had no intention of bringing him in alive, and Boone knew it.

Boone looked from Strykes to the other two men lying dead on the ground. "You got a little carried away, don't you think?" he asked as he raised an eyebrow at him.

Strykes gave him a hard look. "I made sure none of them would come after my family."

Boone nodded. "I'd say you definitely did that."

"You gonna arrest me now?" Strykes asked, fully prepared to shoot Boone in the leg to give himself a head start.

Boone studied him for a time before he spoke. "I can outdraw you," he said, as if guessing Strykes's thoughts.

"Yeah. I forgot," he grumbled.

"Why do you think Travis sent me instead of coming himself?"

Strykes frowned. He wasn't expecting that question. "Guess I never gave it much thought."

Boone gave him a slight grin. "He knew you'd kill them all, and he wouldn't be able to look the other way."

Strykes felt the tension leave him, and all the pieces fell into place. "But you would."

"Not necessarily," Boone said as he looked at Lucas's body. "But I ran with that bastard, and Travis knew I'd see things as justifiable." He looked at Strykes. "He also knew that I knew you. Strykes, you may be a scary son of a bitch, but you're a good man, and I've seen you more than once go up against Lucas and Fisher. If it hadn't been for you, Leslie would have been raped when they had her, and you helped her escape. You saved her life, and I can never thank you enough for that." He cut a glance at the bodies. "I'd say we're even now."

Strykes couldn't help but smile at him as relief washed over him. "I think we're getting soft, Boone."

Boone laughed. "Just don't tell anyone."

Strykes looked past Boone to see Rafe and Logan riding in with the two outlaws who had run. They were unarmed with their hands tied behind their back as the men led their horses along. Hank rode with them, leading Strykes's mare.

"Come on. Let's get the bodies back to town and get home to our wives."

Strykes nodded, and they went about slinging the bodies over the horses and tying them down. Hell yes, he wanted to get home to his wife. He had left her without a word to keep her safe, and he only hoped she would speak to him again. He felt his heart squeeze. Jesus, what if she wanted nothing to do with him now? Maybe it would be better that way. He wouldn't have to worry about hurting her someday. No. Now that he had her, he could never give her up, not even to keep her safe.

Chapter Twenty-Four

Strykes arrived back at the cabin before dawn. He was exhausted, but he didn't want to take the time to rest. The desperate need to get back to LaRisa drove him on. He had been gone for only two days, but it felt like an eternity.

Dismounting, Strykes had a feeling that something was horribly wrong. There was no protective barking from Saber inside. No greeting whinny from Blackie. His eyes went to the corral. In the dim moonlight, he could easily tell it was empty.

Something close to panic seized him, and he rushed into the cabin. "LaRisa?" He was met with cold, empty silence.

Strykes went into the bedroom, hoping to find her sleeping, but the bed was empty, blankets rumpled and askew. Damn, where was she? Had Lucas sent a man after her? No, the cruel bastard would have wanted to hurt her himself.

Rushing from the cabin, Strykes mounted his horse and turned her toward Matthew Reeves's house. If LaRisa had gone anywhere, it would have been to her parents. A place where she felt safe.

The bay horse set into a ground-eating lope she could maintain for miles. Every possible reason for LaRisa's absence went through Strykes's mind. Each scenario only caused him greater anxiety. Was she hurt? Did someone from town come harass her? So many possibilities, and he wouldn't know the answer until he saw LaRisa again.

"Shit," he grumbled as everything became clear. "She thinks I abandoned her."

Until that moment, it hadn't occurred to him she might have interpreted his absence as abandonment. He had left in the middle of the night without a word or even a note explaining things to her. He had been gone for two days, and she was left alone, wondering why.

Had he just destroyed everything they had? In trying to keep her safe, he had unknowingly destroyed his future with her.

The sun was peeking over the horizon as Strykes rode up to the ranch house. Buster barked a warning, but Saber barked happily at him as he dismounted. He bent to scratch the dog behind the ears as he looked around. Nobody stirred around the barn or corrals, as all were still sleeping at this early hour. Taking a deep breath, he stepped up onto the porch. He was raising his hand to knock when the door swung open, and Strykes stared at the business end of a double-barreled shotgun. He took a step back.

"Welcome back, you son of a bitch," Matthew Reeves growled out as he cocked both hammers back.

"Is LaRisa here?"

"Haven't you hurt her enough?" Matthew demanded, his anger barely held in check.

Tim appeared at Matthew's side, his eyes hard. "Want me to get the shovel? I know where we can bury him."

It was clear that Matthew was fighting the urge to blow his head off. "You ran out on her. You don't deserve to have her."

Strykes met his hard eyes. "I left to kill Lucas before he could come after her. I made damn sure he was very dead this time."

"Do you have any idea how much you've hurt her?"

Strykes looked away from Matthew's angry eyes and cursed himself. "I never meant to hurt her, but I had to go." He looked at Matthew again. "I had to leave to keep her safe."

"You told me I could kill you if you hurt her," he snapped as his grip on the shotgun tightened.

"Matthew." Shyfawn was at his side, her hand on his arm. "Don't." She looked at Strykes, her emerald eyes full of compassion. "She's in her room. Go talk to her."

Matthew glared at his wife. "Shyfawn, you can't just welcome him back with open arms after what he's done to her."

She met his hard look evenly. "It's not up to us." She looked at Strykes again. "She's very upset with you. You broke her heart, so don't expect a warm welcome," she told him flatly.

Strykes nodded and swallowed hard. His stomach was twisted in a tight knot, and for a moment he thought he might be sick, but it passed. Shyfawn gestured toward the door, and he took a deep breath before he went into the house. He could feel Matthew's angry eyes on him as he left.

"Guess he'll be staying awhile," Tim said bitterly. "I'll see to his horse." He left the house and led the tired mare to the barn.

"Damn it, Shyfawn," Matthew ground out.

She gave him a small smile. "Everything will work out, Matthew."

"How can you be so sure?"

"They love each other very much." She stood on her toes and gave him a kiss. "Love can do amazing things." She smiled up at him. "You of all people know that."

He looked at her for a long moment, and his expression softened. "Yeah." A smile tugged at his mouth. "You're right." He moved to lean the shotgun against the side of the house, then took her in his arms.

Shyfawn gave a contented sigh and leaned into him as he held her. "Love changed our lives."

"That it did." He took her chin and tipped her face to his. "And I thank God every day for having you." He kissed her softly before he drew back to look at her.

"I'm sure they'll be up there for a while," Shyfawn said with a knowing smile. "Let's go down to the river and give them some privacy."

"The river? It'll be too cold this morning to swim," he pointed out.

"Who said anything about swimming?" she said, a smile playing on her lips.

Matthew smiled back at her and kissed her soundly before he led her down the path to the river.

***

Strykes stopped at the door at the end of the hall and paused. He took a deep breath of courage and raised his hand to knock, then stopped and lowered it. The hour was still early, and she could be sleeping. Should he wait until she was awake before talking to her? He couldn't wait that long.

Carefully, so as to make no sound, he opened the door and slowly pushed it open. LaRisa lay in her bed, her back to him. He closed the door behind him and moved around the bed. When he could see her face, he stopped and stared. She was so damn beautiful, and looking at her nearly stole his breath. Her pale skin, her flaming hair, and the green eyes he so loved were now closed in sleep.

Sitting on the edge of the bed, he watched her sleep. His heart swelled, and he lifted a shaky hand to touch her cheek. Jesus, he had missed her. He had only been away from her for a few days, and he had felt so empty without her. He needed her more than he needed his next breath. His entire existence had been a lonely one until he had shown up on her doorstep, all shot to hell. Now that he'd had a taste of paradise, he couldn't live without it.

LaRisa smiled in her sleep and pressed her cheek to his hand. "Bret." His name came off her lips in a sleepy whisper.

He felt his heart jump, and his throat grew tight. He tilted her head and leaned over to brush his lips lightly over hers. She sighed and brought her hand up to capture the back of his head, pulling him close as she opened her mouth to him.

He obliged her by kissing her deeply, then showered kisses on her face before lightly kissing her lips again. She whispered his name again, and her tone was such that he pulled back to look at her. Her lips trembled and from the corner of her eye, he saw a tear trickle down into the hair at her temple. He swallowed hard and sat up.

She gave a whimper. "Bret, don't leave me again." She rolled away from him and curled into a ball. "You bastard, Strykes."

He couldn't help the smile that tugged at the corners of his mouth. Even in her sleep, she used his last name when she was mad at him. Reaching out, he grabbed her shoulder and laid her on her back. Then he leaned over her and kissed her lightly.

"I'll never leave you again, LaRisa." He told her before he kissed her once more.

At the sound of his voice, her body went stiff, and he pulled back to look at her. Her eyes snapped open, and she blinked up at him. Then she sat bolt upright and scooted away from him, blinking her eyes rapidly as if she were trying to blink away her dream and come back to reality.

"Bret." She gave him a puzzled look. "What're you doing here?"

Strykes wanted to take her in his arms and make love to her, but now was not the time. Standing, he paced to the window, feeling the need to put distance between them before he made love to her anyway. He had to know where he stood with her now. He had to know if she would still want him. Standing there, he watched the sun climb higher in the sky.

"You weren't home when I got there," he told her simply. "I thought you might be here."

"I'm surprised Pa didn't shoot you," she said, honestly wondering how he had gotten past her father.

He turned from the window and looked at her. She sat there on her bed, her hair tousled and her big eyes staring at him expectantly. "He tried, but your ma talked him out of it." She only nodded, seemingly not surprised. "I don't blame him for being mad. He's never liked me much and doesn't like me being with you." He pulled off his hat and worked it in his big hands to hide the fact that they were shaking. "LaRisa, I…" He looked down at his hands. He swore softly and tossed his hat on the bureau to shove his hands in his pockets. "I don't blame you for being mad at me either," he said and looked at her again. "I just…"

She swallowed down the emotion that threatened to choke her. "You left me," she said in an unsteady voice.

"Not like you think," he said as his chest grew tight. "Lucas was alive. I had to go after him before he could hurt you or my sisters."

"So, you left me laying alone in bed while you went to kill him." Her mouth trembled slightly. "Or he could have killed you, and I would have been left wondering why you ran out on me."

"LaRisa, I didn't run out on you." He suddenly felt like a son of a bitch.

"I didn't know that!"

Strykes visibly flinched at the hurt in her voice. "LaRisa, I—"

"I woke up, and you were gone." She felt the tears fall down her cheeks. "You used my body, and you left me!"

He felt as if she had kicked him in the stomach, and for a moment, he couldn't breathe. "Jesus, no. Is that what you think?"

"What the hell was I supposed to think?" she demanded. "You left without a word, and I knew you were never coming back. It was bad enough that the townsfolk don't like me because I'm a witch, but now I'm a jilted wife. Only the lowest sort of woman has a husband that would leave her."

"I was coming back," he told her softly.

"How was I to know that?"

"I'm sorry, LaRisa. I didn't think—"

"No, you didn't!" She couldn't stop the sobs that escaped. "You didn't think to let your wife know you'd be traipsing off to kill someone. To let her know if you didn't come back, it was because you were dead!"

"It had to be done," he snapped, frustration building in him. "How many times do I have to say it before you believe me?"

"Strykes, it doesn't matter if I believe you or not." She didn't bother to fight the tears. "Do you have any idea how much hurt you caused me?"

He marched up to the bed and met her angry gaze with his sorrowful one. "I've been hurting too, damn it. Do you think it was easy for me to leave you that day?"

"It must have been, because you left!"

"LaRisa, I love you!" He knelt next to the bed and looked up at her, his clear blue eyes shining with moisture. "It tore my heart out that day when I left you laying there. I had to do it. I had to go after Lucas."

"You should have asked my opinion before you ran out in the middle of the night." She scooted away from him slightly. He had used her and cast her aside. She wasn't about to give in to him. "But instead, you left without a word."

"I couldn't tell you," he said softly. "You wouldn't have let me go. I had to find Lucas, and I couldn't tell you about it. I'm sorry for doing that."

"Sorry isn't going to fix anything, Strykes!"

He flinched. "I know I can't take away what I did, but I want to make it up to you."

"Make it up to me?" She almost laughed at the words. "What if I don't want you to?" The pain reflected in his eyes nearly killed her. "How do I know you won't get a wild hair and take off again? How do I know there isn't someone else lurking in the shadows that you'll have to run off and kill?" She was trying her hardest not to throw herself into his arms and forgive him, but that was exactly what she wanted to do.

"I would never leave you again." He tried to reach for her, but she jumped off the other side of the bed and faced him.

"How in the hell would I know that?" she demanded.

Strykes got to his feet and stood there on the other side of the bed. She sure as hell wasn't making this easy for him. Not that he blamed her. If she had walked out on him without a word, he wasn't sure if he could forgive her, no matter her reasons. It was easy for him to think he could, but he hadn't gone through the hurt and anger that she had.

"LaRisa, leaving you may be the best thing I could ever do for you," he bit out past the tightness in his throat. "I'm a bastard, and you deserve a better man than me."

She frowned at him and felt her heart break. "Are you going to leave me again?"

"No," he told her flatly. "I could never leave you. I love you, and the few days I was away from you nearly killed me. I couldn't get you off my mind," he said quietly as he looked down at his boots. "I'd close my eyes and see your smile. I heard your laughter on the wind. The green of the leaves reminded me of your eyes. In every sunset, I saw your beautiful hair. Everywhere I looked, there you were. I've missed you so much.

I know I'm no good for you, and I should walk out of your life for your own good."

"What did you miss the most?"

Her question caused him to look at her. "What?"

"What did you miss the most?" she asked again quietly. "It's a simple question."

He looked at her for a long time. She stood there in her thin nightdress, her hands laced together before her, her bare feet shifting uneasily, her hair lying about her shoulders in wavy locks, and her beautiful face staring at him intently. He saw the tears swimming in her eyes and felt his chest squeeze tight.

"Your voice."

She blinked at him. "My voice?"

He nodded. "Yes. I missed the soothing sound of it. The way you talked to me when I was shot, all soft and gentle. The way you'd snap at me when you were mad. The way you'd sing when you thought I couldn't hear you. The everyday conversation we shared in the cabin after we were married."

"My voice," she said again, as if she didn't believe him. "You missed my voice?"

"What did you want me to say?" He didn't care if it wasn't the answer she wanted, but it was the truth. "I miss everything about you, but your voice always let me know you were there, that you were with me." He gave a heaving sigh and sank down on the edge of the bed and put his head in his hands. "I love you, and I'm sorry. I left, and it hurt you, but I had to kill Lucas before he tried to take you from me. I can't make it without you, LaRisa," he told her and suddenly realized just how true that statement was. He had never needed anyone before, but he desperately needed her.

LaRisa looked at the big man seated on her bed and felt the tears falling down her cheeks. Strykes had poured his heart out to her and begged forgiveness. He had said nothing of missing her body or the passion they had shared. He told her he had missed *her*; he loved her for who she was. That meant more to her than he would ever know.

She stepped around the bed and knelt before him. Taking his face in her hands, she forced him to look at her. His eyes were filled with pain and sorrow; his cheeks were wet with tears. She choked on a sob and wiped the tears away from his cheeks with her thumbs. How many times had he done that for her?

"I love you too, and I forgive you." She could barely get the words out. "You're my husband, and I want you to be with me forever."

Strykes muttered something and pulled her against him. Her body shook with sobs as she cried into his chest. His body shuddered from the pure emotion that ripped through him. He pulled back and kissed her, their tears mingling together.

Chapter Twenty-Five

LaRisa looked at Strykes and reached up to stroke her hand along his whiskered jaw. He looked tired. He must have been relentless in tracking Lucas down. She didn't have to ask to know it had been brutal. She could feel the repercussions of what he had done buried inside him. He didn't like to kill, but he was good at it, and it had to be done. He had killed a cruel man to protect his family. But there was a deeper pain in him, one she had felt before but didn't understand.

She bit her lip as she opened his shirt and placed her palm over his heart. Why was the buried pain in him so much stronger than before? She closed her eyes and let her energy flow. She wasn't afraid, and there was no self-doubt as she eased the buried pain inside Strykes.

The air left Strykes in a rush as he felt her hand heat, and a strange feeling washed over him. A calm settled in him, and it felt as if the years of anger, guilt, and hatred vanished. There was no worry, no regret, and no fear. He felt as if she were caressing his very soul. A soul he thought he had lost long ago.

"LaRisa," he breathed her name as he covered her hand with his.

She opened her eyes, and he stared into their emerald depths. He saw the tears shimmering in them and felt his own eyes burn. He lowered his mouth to hers and kissed her. His hands moved to cup her face as his mouth teased gently over hers before he kissed her deeply. After a moment, he pulled back to rest his forehead against hers. He took a breath and placed his hand over hers again.

"Are you all right?" she asked softly.

He drew back and smiled at her. "I am now." He took a deep breath and let it out slowly. "I'm not sure what you just did, but I've never felt better."

"I-I've never done that before." She looked at her hand on his chest. "You were hurting," she whispered. "You have so much pain hidden inside you."

He studied her for a moment. "You can feel it?"

She nodded. "What happened?"

He said nothing for a long time. "Things you don't want to know about." He told her honestly. "A lot of death, LaRisa."

She bit her lip for a moment and held his gaze. "Murder?"

He said nothing, but she could almost see him thinking back over his past.

"They don't call it murder in war," he said simply.

"What about Lucas?" she asked with dread.

"Not really." He saw the worry in her eyes and pulled her close. "He was a wanted man, and there was a price on his head. Travis deputized Boone and sent him after me. I won't lie. We had one hell of a fight with Lucas and his men, and in the end, almost all of them died. Even if Boone hadn't been there, I would have killed them all. I wasn't going to let one of them live to come back and threaten your life."

LaRisa absently stroked her fingers over his muscular chest. She knew there was a lot more to his story and he would never tell her, but it didn't matter. Nothing mattered anymore. He was here with her, and he would never leave her again. Would he?

She felt the tears burn her eyes as she drew back to look at him. "Is it finally safe for us?"

He gave her a small smile. "Yes, LaRisa. It's finally safe." He took her hand and brought it to his mouth to kiss her palm. "We can go home and not have to worry about some bastard lurking in the shadows. I want to go home, LaRisa. I want to go to our home where we can be together and spend the rest of my life loving you."

She couldn't speak, so she kissed him. Her heart was so full she thought it might burst. He loved her, and he was with her again. They were safe, and nothing would come between them ever again. She kissed him deeply as her hands pulled at his shirt. He helped her remove it and groaned when her hands splayed across his chest.

"I was so afraid I'd never see you again," she said through her tears.

He took her face in his hands and looked into her emerald eyes. "Nothing could keep me from coming back, LaRisa. I love you, and I'll spend every day for the rest of my life proving it to you."

He gently kissed her tears away before he claimed her mouth for a deep, stirring kiss. He poured every ounce of love he felt for her into the kiss, and she kissed him back just as passionately. In record time, he had shed them of their clothes and had her beneath him on the bed. He urged her legs apart, and she eagerly accommodated him. He pushed inside her with one deep thrust. She cried out, and he groaned through clenched teeth.

"God, LaRisa," he growled as he tried to get even deeper inside her.

She moved her body against him, and he swore. He levered over her and set a strong slow rhythm that had her crying out and writhing beneath him. Jesus, he loved her, and nothing was going to take him away from her again. He would walk through hell to protect her and kill any man who got in his way.

"Bret," she cried, and he felt her tighten around his shaft.

Strykes shifted over her, and his thrust became more forceful. She wrapped her long legs around his hips, and her nails bit into his back as her pleasure grew. He gritted his teeth and groaned out a curse as she tightened painfully around him, threatening to take him over the edge.

Only when she screamed his name and her body shattered as her release came did he allow his own pleasure to take him. He gave his own harsh cry as his body went rigid, and he emptied himself deep inside her. Her body pulsed and gripped his shaft, as if trying to take every drop he had. He collapsed over her, his breathing ragged. He held her close until their bodies stopped shaking and their breathing slowed.

Strykes lifted his head and looked at her. She gave him a small smile, her eyes bright with passion and tears. He kissed her gently before he rolled off her and gathered her close to hold her tight. She let out a contented sigh, and he placed a kiss on her damp forehead.

"God, I've missed you," she said, and he couldn't help but smile at the satisfied bliss in her voice.

"I've missed you too." His arms tightened around her. "I can't wait to get home and get back to being your devoted husband," he told her as he let his hand drift down over her body.

She laughed softly and nestled against him. Then she felt her heart sink. He was going to be more than just a husband now. "Bret."

"Yeah." He felt a change in her. "What is it?"

She bit her lip for a moment. "Th-there's something I need to tell you."

Something in her voice made him ease back to look at her. "LaRisa?" He studied her face and saw the worry there. "What's wrong?"

"Bret, I…" She swallowed hard. "We're…" She felt the tears fill her eyes.

"LaRisa, honey." He laid her back and lifted up on an elbow to lean over her. "Talk to me." He stroked a hand along her cheek.

"Bret." Emotion clogged her throat, and she fought to find her voice. She took his hand and moved it to her stomach. "Bret, we're going to have a baby." She felt his body tense, and his energy shifted violently.

LaRisa wasn't sure what kind of reaction to expect from him, but his complete silence made her heart stop. He only stared at her with those pale-blue eyes. His look of shock changed into something she had never seen in his eyes before. Fear. His eyes moved to her stomach, and he swallowed hard. He slowly eased his hand from her stomach, and she couldn't stop the sob that escaped.

"Bret." She could hardly choke the words out. "It'll be all right."

She watched through her tears as he drew away from her and sat up. He only stared at her; his face held worry and fear. She sat up and faced him, her own fear nearly choking her. He appeared to be fighting for air as his eyes drifted to her stomach.

"Bret, it'll be all right," she cried. "I won't kill him. I'll wear gloves all the time."

His eyes flew to hers, and she read the shock there. "What?"

"I promise," she sobbed, and her tears fell freely. "I'll wear gloves all the time."

"LaRisa—"

"I won't touch him with my bare hands." She looked at her hands for a moment. "I won't kill him. I'll wear my gloves. I'll be careful not to touch him. I won't kill him."

He grabbed her by the shoulders. "LaRisa," he snapped, and her eyes lifted to his. "Jesus, is that what you think?"

She nodded. "You don't have to be afraid I'll hurt him. I'll wear gloves. I won't kill…" Her voice choked off as she cried.

Strykes swore and lifted her into his lap as he held her close. "Honey, don't think like that. You'd never hurt our baby."

"But you looked afraid," she said through her sobs.

Strykes took a deep breath and stroked a hand over her hair as he cradled her head to his shoulder. "I am afraid, LaRisa," he confessed. "But not of you hurting our baby. I'm…I'm afraid *I* will."

She shifted against him and looked up at him. "What? I don't understand."

He gave her a soft smile as he brushed her tears away. "I guess there's a few things you need to know."

She sniffed and looked at him through her tears. "Tell me."

Strykes took a deep breath. "I've never talked about my family for a reason," he told her hesitantly. "You've met Skye and Willow."

"And I like them very much," she said.

"They are sweet. So is Ashton." He settled his arms around her and held her close. "Our mother was a fine, gentle woman, and we all loved her." He said nothing for a moment. "Our father was a complete son of a bitch."

"Tell me," she coaxed when he had gone silent.

"He'd hit our ma, and he'd beat the hell out of me," he reluctantly told her. "One day he hit her, and he wouldn't stop. I tried to stop him, but he started beating me. He would have killed me if Ashton hadn't hit him on the head with a shovel. She knocked him out cold, but it was too late. He had killed our ma."

"Oh, Bret." She felt new tears fall down her cheeks.

"He'd beat me bloody every chance he got. But one day I was big enough I fought back. I knocked him down, and he never hit me again." He was quiet for a moment as he thought back. "I found him beating Willow in the barn one day. She was thirteen and so small. I didn't even stop to think. I lit in the middle of him, and we had one hell of a fight. He shot me, and I broke his neck."

LaRisa couldn't stop the gasp that escaped her. "Bret." She reached out and touched his face.

"I'm like him, LaRisa," he told her in an unsteady voice. "I look just like the bastard, and I have so many of his traits it scares me. If I ever hurt you…" He let his gaze drift to her stomach, and he placed a big hand over their child. "If I ever hurt our children…"

"You won't," she told him firmly as she placed her hand over his and waited for him to look at her. "You're not your father. You would never hurt us."

"LaRisa, you can't be sure of that. I told your pa what could happen when he wanted us to marry," he told her regretfully. "I told him I could hurt you or even kill you someday." He swallowed hard and looked down at his hand over her stomach so she wouldn't see the moisture in his eyes. "After waking up with a rifle pointed at my forehead, I knew I could count on your pa."

"What do you mean?" She stroked a hand through his hair and wished he would look at her.

He caressed their child and fought down the emotion that made his chest tight. "I told him if I ever raised a hand to you, I wanted him to kill me. It didn't surprise me when he agreed without hesitation."

LaRisa gasped, and her mouth fell open in shock. "Jesus."

She couldn't breathe for a moment, then her shock gave way to anger. She wound her fingers in his hair and jerked back until he was forced to look at her. His eyes were wet with tears and held fear and sorrow. She suddenly understood the deeply buried pain inside him. He was scared to death he would hurt her or their children. She now understood what he meant when he had told her he wasn't a good man and she deserved someone better. Every day he was with her, he was afraid he would hurt her, and it was eating him up inside.

"You are not your father," she snapped at him. "You hate him so much you'd never let yourself become him. You protected your sisters, and you've protected me. You won't hurt me, and you won't hurt our children." She didn't bother to blink back her tears as they filled her eyes. "Stop being afraid of who you're not and be who you are." Her tears spilled from her eyes as his own found freedom.

Strykes couldn't speak as he looked at her, and her words washed over him. She was right. He had spent his life hating his father and lived in fear of being like him someday. Strykes had done a lot of things he wasn't proud of, but he had never hurt a woman, and he would beat any man who did. He would move heaven and hell to keep LaRisa safe. He had even made sure there was someone willing to kill him if he hurt her. She was right. He wasn't his father, and he never would be. He had never been truly happy until he'd met LaRisa, and with her he could be himself, be the man he wanted to be. Finally, he could be the man he truly was, all because of her.

"Don't be afraid of hurting me, because you won't. You never could hurt our children, so don't even think like that," she told him firmly. "I'll knock you in the head next time you have that thought."

He looked at her as she scowled at him, her hand wound painfully in his hair to be sure he held her eyes. Jesus, he loved her. He couldn't stop the small chuckle that escaped him. "Are you always going to be this forceful?"

She blinked at him, then gave him a small smile. "Only when I have to be." She kept a hold of his hair and kissed him. "And don't you forget it," she said against his mouth before kissing him again.

Strykes wrapped his arms around her and pulled her close to kiss her back. She released his hair and took his face in her hands. She kissed him until they were breathless and then rested her forehead to his. They stayed like that for a long time before he took her hands and leaned back to look at them. He kissed each palm gently and looked at her.

"I won't have you thinking you'll hurt our children either," he told her flatly and smiled at her. "I'll knock you in the head next time you have that thought," he said, repeating her words back to her.

She smiled at him and felt the new flow of tears. "You do"—she held her palm up to him—"and I'll suck the life right out of you."

He chuckled and kissed her softly. "I think we're going to be just fine, honey."

"I love you, Bret," she told him as she caressed his jaw.

He laid her back on the bed and pressed a kiss to her stomach. "I love you." He drew back and brushed his hand over their child. "I never thought I'd ever be in love, be a husband, or be a father." He moved over her and rested on his elbows as he looked at her. "But I found you, and I swear I fell in love the first time I saw you."

She blinked back her tears and smiled at him. "I confess I felt the same way. I was scared of you a little at first, but after you danced with me at Leslie and Boone's wedding, I wanted to see more of you."

He grinned at her. "Is that why you kept your horse in new shoes all the time?"

She laughed and nodded. "I was hoping you wouldn't notice."

He chuckled. "Hell yes, I noticed. I only wished you had more horses."

She laughed and drew his head down to kiss him.

There was a knock at the door, and they both froze. LaRisa's heart pounded. They were both very naked and very much tangled up together.

"You two better get dressed and come get some breakfast," Shyfawn said, and they heard the humor in her voice.

"We'll be right there, Mama," LaRisa answered and tried not to laugh at the blush she saw creep up Strykes's neck.

"At least it wasn't your pa. He'd kill me for doing this with his daughter in his house."

She smiled brightly. "Don't worry; I wouldn't let him. Come on, let's go have breakfast."

Strykes rolled off her, and they gathered their clothes to dress. He watched her slip into her dress and felt his heart swell with love. A family. Never in his life had he ever thought he would be a family man. The thought had always terrified him before, but LaRisa had changed all that for him.

She opened the door, and he put a hand on her arm to stop her. He looked at her for a long time before he drew her close and kissed her gently. She sighed and leaned into him. This was what he had longed to have for so many years.

She drew back and looked up at him. "Are you all right?"

He nodded and caressed her cheek. "I am now."

Epilogue

Strykes stood in the parlor of the new dress shop in town. His sisters had settled in and had a prosperous business going. He looked down at his new dark-blue shirt. It was a perfect fit. His eyes lifted to LaRisa as she sat in the rocker with their three-month-old son and smiled. She was wearing that new dress he had promised her. His sisters had made her a beautiful green dress that accented her eyes.

LaRisa looked up and smiled at him. "Are you going to stand there all day just staring at us?"

He nodded. "I'll never tire of looking at you."

LaRisa brushed her bare hand over the head of their sleeping son. All fear of hurting their child had vanished the instant he was born. Her love for him erased her fears, and she never wore gloves when she held him. She never wore her gloves at all anymore.

Strykes, too, no longer feared. The moment he held his newborn son in his arms, a love so deep washed over him, and everything protective in him surfaced. This was his family, and he wouldn't let anything or anyone hurt them.

A strong knock sounded on the door. Strykes frowned and turned to look at the door. The shop was closed for the day. Willow came scampering from the kitchen with a big smile on her face, and

Strykes had to stifle a groan. He knew who was out there.

Willow flung open the door and greeted Logan McCord with a happy smile. "You're just in time."

She stepped back and let Logan enter, and Rafe Reeves followed him inside. They offered a greeting to Strykes, and after a glare from Willow, he muttered a greeting of his own. Once again, the two young men were having dinner with his sisters. He knew he should have killed them.

They came to call on his sisters often. Though Skye didn't encourage Rafe like Willow did Logan, the man still came to see her. His sisters were grown women, and he knew they would court and get married one day, but he wasn't ready for that yet.

"Come sit at the table," Willow ordered and shooed the men toward the dining room.

Strykes went into the parlor to see LaRisa up and walking their sleeping son across the floor. "Time to eat."

She nodded and walked to him. He stopped her to kiss her gently before he took their son from her. A small fussing sound left him as he stretched before settling into Strykes's arms.

They went to the dining room and sat. Strykes cradled his son in one arm to leave his other hand free to eat.

Strykes looked at his family and didn't think he could get any happier. He had a wife and child, and his sisters were with him. A shadow fell over his heart. They had never received word from Ashton. Strykes didn't know what had happened in New Orleans. Whenever he brought it up, Skye would burst into tears, and Willow refused to talk about it.

Having the dress shop was good for Skye. Her sparkle was still gone, but she was becoming less withdrawn. Rafe sat beside her and did his best to make conversation, but she didn't engage, only giving him one-word answers to any question he asked her. Willow, on the other hand, was a chatterbox. She talked with everyone present, but her attention was focused on Logan.

LaRisa reached over and placed her hand on his thigh. He looked at her and gave her a soft smile. He placed his hand over hers and held it gently.

There was no longer room in their lives for fear. It had been replaced with love. A love that would only grow along with his family.

To my readers,
    If you enjoyed this book,
please consider leaving a
review at your favorite book
store.
    All reviews are much
appreciated.
    Thank you.
    T.K. Conklin

Books by T.K. Conklin

Rimrock Series
Promise of Tomorrow
Promise of Spring

Wild Love Series
Outlaw's Redemption
Guarded Hearts
Threads of Passion

Keep in touch with T.K.
Facebook
Twitter
Instagram